Bleed Black

Rebecca L. Kershaw
x

Rebecca L. Kershaw

Pen Press

First published in Great Britain

All paper used in the printing of this book has been made from wood grown in managed, sustainable forests.

ISBN13: 978-1-78003-444-7

Printed and bound in the UK
Pen Press is an imprint of
Indepenpress Publishing Limited
25 Eastern Place
Brighton
BN2 1GJ

A catalogue record of this book is available from
the British Library

Cover design by Jacqueline Abromeit

Part One

Litha

Chapter One

1993

I stood at the door of the common room, my blazer stiff with newness, hands clenched inside my pockets and I knew they were all going to hate me. I longed for the anonymity of my suburban high school, for the friends I'd had since nursery and the familiar smell of the 1960s building. This school was far smaller, only a village school. I'd pleaded with my parents to let me start at the big comprehensive in town, but instead they sent me here, to the neat red brick and the tidy hedges. It even smelled different, freshly mown grass and new paint. I longed for asphalt and sweat. Oh they were definitely going to hate me, I could tell as I hesitated on the threshold of the common room. And I was going to hate them.

'Sod this.' I swung round and walked straight into the most beautiful girl I'd ever met.

'Hey, slow down, are you trying to flatten me?' She caught hold of my arm to balance herself and I found myself looking into calm grey eyes in a face framed by sweeps of black hair.

'I'm sorry,' I mumbled and made to walk past.

'You must be the new boy. David.'

'Yeah.' God the teachers must have told them all about me, asked them to keep an eye out for me and all I wanted was to be nameless.

'You've moved into Verger's Cottage, in the village.'

Had they broadcast my entire history?

'We watched you move in last week.'

I raised my eyebrows, 'We?'

'Me and my boyfriend. He lives in the Old Vicarage next door to you.'

I knew the Old Vicarage. You couldn't miss it, one of those houses books describe as 'rambling', with Victorian gables and porches everywhere and a garden filled with dogs and roses. There were three or four cars and a boat on a trailer drawn up on the driveway. Whoever her boyfriend was he had money. And a fit girlfriend.

The fit girlfriend looked at me as if she expected me to comment or something but when I remained silent she shrugged and held out her hand. I took it, feeling her heavy silver ring against my palm.

'I'm Celia. See you around.' She dropped my hand and pushed open the common room door. Then, over her shoulder, 'By the way there's a start of year party at The Plough on Friday. You should come.'

I already knew that the last thing I was going to do on Friday night was go to a party in the local pub. I'd seen enough of the kids at school to know what it would be like. They'd have parents drop them off in 4x4s that were actually used on farms and they'd have clothes that were too nice to be cool. They'd drink too much in a really loud way. And they wouldn't notice if I was there or not. They would care less.

On my way home, though, I looked more closely at the Old Vicarage, wondering if I'd see sexy Celia again, visiting her boyfriend. There was no sign of life, just a couple of sheets moving listlessly on the clothes line between the apple trees, and an open window on the second floor.

Friday night and half an hour of listening to my parents bickering in their bedroom was enough to make a party with the Country Life set seem appealing. I really didn't need another night of agonising over whose fault it was we'd ended up in a leaky cottage, in the dullest village on earth, whilst I tried to organise my CDs on a couple of warped and sagging shelves. I thought nostalgically about my steel floor to ceiling shelving, left behind because it wouldn't fit under this stupid sloping roof.

The bedroom door slammed and Mum went stomping down the stairs. The party it was. One thing though. If I was going, it would be as myself, with no trying to fit in, no conforming to their expectations. If they were going to hate me, they might as well hate the real me.

Back home there'd been a whole group of us who hung together, listened to the same music, watched the same films and dressed in the same clothes. Which meant we wore black. All the time. It was meant to be a statement or something and it felt good. Dad called us a coterie of crows but there was anonymity in the crowd. That was the last thing I could expect tonight. Tonight I'd be the only goth in the village. I was going to hate it but I was going to do it. In protest. Protest against this village, this house, my mum and dad for bringing me here. Against all the people at this stupid party who I didn't even know.

I pulled on black jeans, T-shirt and jacket, gelled my hair into little spikes and searched for my eyeliner pencil. When I'd finished I recognised myself in the mirror for the first time since we left Newcastle.

The arguing had started again upstairs so Dad's whisky was unguarded in the sideboard. I took two quick swigs, waiting for the smoky hit in the back of my throat, wiped my mouth on the back of my hand and left the house.

Walking through the early September evening I wondered how there could be a back to school party at a pub? Hadn't they heard of ID cards? I didn't know the countryside then. There was nowhere else to go and the back room of The Plough was always booked out for seventeenth and eighteenth birthday parties. At the door I hesitated. Should I just walk in through the bar? Was there a back entrance? I wasn't ready to face a barful of locals. A Range Rover pulled up to let out two girls with short skirts and tans. They headed off round the side of the pub and I followed, ignoring their curious glances.

Fortunately the room was dark. That was the only positive. Otherwise this party was everything I'd dreaded. A bunch of girls, who looked exactly like the ones from the Range Rover, were dancing, flicking long hair and drinking from bottles. Everybody else was lined around the walls, watching me through the laser cuts of strobe effects. Even in the dim lighting I could see that trendy shirts and smart haircuts were in. People were swigging Pimms without irony. Not a trace of goth anywhere. I tried to back out of the room but there were more smart haircuts coming in behind me and I was pushed out onto the dancefloor.

'Watch it!' One of the dancers pushed me back and glared.

'Sorry,' I muttered and made for the shadows of the far wall, where I prayed for a bar and a barman who would serve me. As I crossed the room it felt like the floor was being stretched out like well chewed chewing gum and I'd have to keep walking forever while everyone watched and the bar endlessly receded. A longing to belong again stabbed my guts. I wasn't meant to be here. Misery welled up and I nearly bolted.

'Hi, David. You came.' I swung round, then almost swung back. There could be a dozen David's here. But it was Celia, leaning on the bar with a pint glass in her hand and smiling at me. She was all in black with her long hair over her face. I smiled in relief.

'Hi. Yeah. I came. Wish I hadn't though. Not really my scene.'

'I wouldn't say that. Apart from me and Celia I'd say you were the best dressed here.' A tall, slim bloke unfolded himself from a barstool and extended a hand. He was dressed head to toe in black. He was wearing eyeliner.

'Pleased to meet you, David. I'm Ash. Can I get you a drink?'

Can you fall in love in the splintering of a second? I looked at Celia and Ash and it felt like you could.

So, that's how it started. And as easy as that, I had two new best friends and a school full of would be friends. Ash Fitzpatrick thought I was cool, so cool I must be. And I'd put so much effort into not fitting in.

Ash's dad owned a boatyard in Seahouses and the sea was Ash's second home. A couple of days after the party he took me out in his dinghy. Without the makeup and black clothes he looked more ordinary but I could see why all the girls fancied him and the boys wanted to be him. Everything he did was effortless. From launching the boat off the short slipway to swinging himself aboard and unfurling the sails as we followed the wind out onto the bay, he did it all smoothly, gracefully, as if none of it really mattered. As soon as he had us on a steady heading he lit a cigarette and cracked open a bottle of beer.

'Smoke, beer?'

I declined and accepted and settled on the hard seat in the stern. Ash kept his eyes on the horizon and one hand on the tiller.

'You're living next door then? Where the old bloke died? We watched you moving in.'

'Yeah, Celia said.' I took a mouthful of beer and dodged a plume of spray as Ash adjusted course. 'It seems a bit quiet round here. After Newcastle anyway.'

'City boy? You'll think it's dead here. It doesn't bother me. There's a good pub, the sea's on my doorstep and we go into town to see bands and stuff. I couldn't live in the city. No sky.'

'Have you always lived in the village then?'

'Nah. I moved here when I was twelve. My parents split up and Mum got a new boyfriend.' He raised his eyebrows. 'So I came to live with Dad and Kate.'

'Kate?'

'His second wife. She's cool. Caroline, my kid sister, moved in a couple of months ago. She's pissed off with Mum as well.'

I nodded. 'Do you see your mum much?'

'No.' He did something complicated with the sails and I had to duck quickly as we came around. As soon as we were on a straight course again he opened another beer, and sailed for the horizon.

After a bit I tried again, 'What about Celia?'

'What about her?'

'Well, does she come from round here? Have you two been together long?'

He gave me a long, considering look. Then he smiled.

'Celia's dad used to be the crossings man, in the next village, before they went automated. Celia's lived in the railway house since she was a little girl. Her dad died when she was thirteen so it's just her and her mum now.'

'And you two?'

'Oh, we've been together forever.'

They'd actually been together about two years by the time I met them but everyone agreed it might as well have been forever.

'It was like something out of a novel,' one of the girls told me. We'd already established that she was in love with Ash. 'Her dad died and she changed schools. She came up to the classroom door at the same time as Ash and they just looked at each other and he sat with her and that was it. Like it was just meant to be.' She rolled her eyes. 'Romeo and bloody Juliet.'

'She was the right age,' I said but the girl had walked away.

For months I held my breath, certain Ash and Celia would tire of me; waiting for the invitations to dry up. Probably everyone else expected it too. But it didn't happen. It never happened.

I'd thought it was fairly obvious but when Ash found out how I felt about Celia it provoked our first row.

The three of us were walking along the beach near Embleton. Ash had borrowed his dad's old Volvo and we parked up on the headland. Ash and Celia were hand in hand and I was walking at a distance from them, skimming stones into the creamy waves. It was a windy day, the sand whipped up and thrown in our faces, gusts tugging at Celia's skirts and streaming her hair behind her like a raven flag. The wind must have got too strong for her because she turned away from Ash and, head bent against the wind, made her way back up the beach to the car park. Halfway she turned and blew a kiss towards us. He blew a kiss back and I waved.

He turned to me and said, 'She is beautiful isn't she?'

For once I forgot myself and breathed, 'Gorgeous. If you two ever split up I'll be first in line.'

I think I was joking but I didn't have time to decide because Ash had me by the throat. His fingers were like steel pincers against my windpipe squeezing tighter and tighter. As shock gave way to anger I started to struggle, twisting desperately against his grip, knowing he had twice my strength. I tried to prise his fingers away from my throat with one hand and forced the other under his chin, pushing his head back. I kicked out recklessly and connected with his shin bone. He yelled out and let me go. I staggered away, rubbing my throat, drawing great ragged breaths.

The next I knew he was behind me, one arm across my throat, the other twisting my arm up my back, 'If you ever so much as look at Celia like that, if you even breathe on her. If you ever – ever'. He twisted my arm even higher and his forearm crushed my windpipe. In a fog of pain I thought I was going to pass out. 'If you ever even talk about trying it on with Celia I will fucking kill you. I will rip that clever fucking head off those clever fucking shoulders'. His body was shaking, way out of control. Then as suddenly as it had started it was over and he let go. He pushed me away and I staggered, clutching my throat. I watched him take three or four deep breaths, bend to fling a handful of pebbles into the waves and then, without looking at me, head back across the beach. Pride told me to let him go but we were miles from home so, still shaken, I followed.

When we reached the car he smiled briefly at Celia, waiting in the passenger seat and, with a jerk of his thumb, motioned me into the back. We drove home in strained silence, yet Celia never once asked what had happened.

I didn't see Ash for three or four days after that. His dad took him and Celia away to a boat sale in Scotland and I had too much time to think. Maybe I'd deserved his reaction. I was terrified he was going to blank me. When he got back I literally ran into him in the grassy passage between our houses. Suddenly dry mouthed I faced him, ready to start apologising. But before I could speak he waved a hand towards his house.

'Do you want to have a look at the brochures I picked up at the sale? And I thought we might go for a pint later.'

There wasn't a trace of awkwardness or hostility, he was just careless, charming Ash. The scene on the beach might never have happened. I swallowed my over prepared apology and followed him into the house, relieved but, somehow, disappointed.

After that I started to watch out for his moods. I realised that his dark side was only lightly cloaked. Celia knew it too and occasionally I caught her watching him with questions in her eyes.

I don't know why I was so surprised when I found out Celia was a Christian. I knew she wore a big silver cross but I thought that was an image thing. We were walking her home one night, across the fields.

It was early on in our friendship and it must have been a Saturday because Ash asked, 'Am I meeting you from church tomorrow?'

I was going to laugh. I mean nobody our age went to church. But Celia just said 'Yes – about 12 o'clock.' And they kept on walking.

'Do you go to church often then?' I didn't want to sound like I was taking the piss but she didn't seem to mind.

'Yeah, every week. Didn't you know?'

I wanted to ask her what she went for, why she needed to but it wasn't the right time.

I asked Ash later and he said it was no big deal. Celia was a Christian, end of story.

'It's nice that she prays for me.' He was joking then but he certainly needed her prayers later on.

'But what about sex? Aren't Christians into the whole no sex before marriage thing?' I wouldn't normally have asked but we were both pissed, so what the hell.

He smiled and said, 'What the fuck's it got to do with you?' But he told me anyway. 'She's part of me and I love her, all of her. Sex or no sex.' I didn't know whether I believed him but it was the only answer I was going to get.

So that's how it was. And whatever the reasons we became inseparable. It was always Ash, Celia and David. I wanted it to stay that way forever. But things were already changing. We were at the end of our school careers, university loomed. We had it all planned though. When we'd got our degrees Ash and Celia would get married and we'd all move back to the village. I think we believed it. I certainly did. Maybe it could have happened but we'd never know. Because right at the end of the school year, at the start of the summer, Angel came.

Chapter Two

I met Angel at 4 o'clock on a Friday afternoon. Exams were over and I was waiting for Ash and Celia in the deserted common room. I'd wasted half the afternoon already, going through college applications with Ash. He hadn't a clue what course he wanted to do, as long as it was in the same city as me and Celia. Now he'd wandered off to get Celia from the art room and all I wanted to do was go home and start the weekend. 'I need a pint,' I muttered, wandering over to the noticeboard, stuck with brightly coloured bits of paper promising a 'great nite' at the chess club party and a stapler amnesty at the end of term. I checked my watch again just as the door opened and Celia walked in. She was talking to someone over her shoulder.

'About time,' I said before I realised it wasn't Ash following behind but a girl I'd never seen before. I ignored the girl and asked Celia, 'Where's Ash? He went looking for you.'

'Hi, David. Nice to see you too.' She gave me one of her 'behave' glares and said, 'He'll find me. Anyway, I want you to meet Angel. She's just moved in near you.'

What sort of a name is Angel, my first thought. Then she looked right at me, without a smile, but with her soul in her eyes and I knew it was the only possible name.

'Angel.' I don't think I said anything else. I'm pretty sure I stared.

'David,' she smiled, half mocking.

Angel left just before Ash turned up and we went on with our evening as if nothing had happened.

We were halfway home from The Plough before I had to ask, 'Who's that Angel girl you were with?'

Ash was trying to kiss the back of Celia's neck and she was making out she wanted him to stop. I certainly did.

'That girl Angel you introduced me to. Who is she?'

'She's Angel,' said Ash, lifting Celia's hair off her neck and twisting it round his fingers as they walked. 'Stupid sort of name though.'

'I like it,' said Celia and I'd never agreed with her more. 'She's just moved into the village and she'll be in the upper sixth next year. The Head wanted her to come in for the last couple of weeks and meet a few people.'

'Not much point meeting you.' Ash bit her ear and I looked away. 'Unless you're going to come and do resits with me, you won't be around next year.'

'You won't be doing resits.' Celia was annoyed and pulled away. 'She only met me 'cos she came to the art room. I like her. She's different.'

We reached my gate and Ash and Celia walked on to his house, leaving me stranded.

I watched them crossing the grass square, his arm snaking round her waist again and I called out, 'Where does she live?'

'At the old Hall,' Celia called back and they disappeared into the gloom of the porch.

I went in, bypassing my parents in the sitting room and ran straight upstairs. We were going out again later, taking the bus into town and I had about an hour to get ready and have something to eat. I could have shouted down to Mum to make me a sandwich and she'd have grumbled but complied. Instead I jumped in the shower and turned the power head on. The jets of water exploded against my skin like tiny grenades. I shut my eyes, letting the water explore my face. It was a long time since I'd thought about any girl other than Celia. When I did have girlfriends I thought about them only to compare with her. Their hair wasn't as long or as shiny. Their breasts were smaller or bigger. They didn't wear black. They didn't live by the railway line. Now I shut my eyes and whispered 'Angel.' It was the best word in the language. 'Angel.' In the hot steam I thought of white wings and golden hair. Then I started thinking of thin white dresses which became see through and I pictured narrow waists and long, smooth legs and breasts which were just like Celia's only they were Angel's. I was getting a hard on and about to slip my hand down when there was a thump on the bathroom door.

'Are you trying water torture in there?' Dad didn't approve of long, hot showers. Apparently they dried the skin and turned the tiles black. I reached for the shampoo.

After that Angel was, in the words of the song, always on my mind. I decided I'd go into school every day to keep Ash company among the applications and I'd visit Celia in the art room to see how the portfolio was getting on. I didn't see Angel once.

I heard plenty about her though. The lower sixth were buzzing about the new girl.

'She's like really weird. I mean you can tell from her clothes. And she lived in a commune! In Wales!'

'My dad says her dad is setting up a commune here and there'll be loads of drugs and stuff.'

'Excellent!'

'Her dad's Lord Hedley's son but I bet he doesn't know they've taken over the Hall. And did you see what she was wearing yesterday – like a bloody rainbow.'

'I thought it was really pretty.'

'Yeah you would. But she'll not talk to you anyway.'

'No she only talks to Celia Lambert.'

'She probably just fancies Ash.'

'Don't we all.'

For once I wished being upper sixth didn't mean I had to avoid talking to the lower sixth whenever possible. I wanted to know everything they could tell me about Angel. I'd only seen her once but already I could conjure her at will, skirts flowing in a stream of colourful fabrics, hair caught up in an Indian scarf, watchful green eyes silently laughing at me. The rumours fuelled my fantasy and I still hadn't seen her again.

I knew Celia was seeing Angel and I was jealous – of both of them. Celia had never really had a close female friend before but now she was always mentioning that she'd met Angel in the art room and, 'We both like modern abstracts.' Or they'd been for coffee in the canteen or met on the way into school. It beat me how they always met when I was somewhere else. Ash didn't like it either. Whenever Celia mentioned that she'd seen Angel he rolled his eyes and said something like, 'Is there something you want to tell me?' Celia just laughed.

Eventually I tried to force the issue. We were at Ash's, waiting for him to get the Land Rover keys, so we could drive into Alnwick. Celia was sitting on the edge of the wall outside the house, kicking her heels against the mossy stones.

'You and this Angel seem to be getting on alright,' I said.

'I like her. She's not like the other girls.'

'She lives at the Hall then?'

'Yeah, I told you she did.' She peered over my shoulder to see if Ash was coming.

'Does her family live there?'

'Well she's not on her own is she?' Celia laughed as Ash came loping towards us, waving the keys.

'Right, we off?' And as we crossed to the Land Rover, 'When we going to meet your new friend then, Celia? The famous Angel. I need to weigh up the competition.'

'David's already met her.' She gave me a sly smile. 'But I've invited her to the pub tomorrow night.'

Chapter Three

I didn't tell my parents anything important. Certainly nothing about girls. But I found myself telling them about Angel. They were washing up after dinner and the kitchen was crowded with the three of us. I lounged against the worktop and obstructed the cupboards as Dad tried to put the pots away.

'She's from the Hall.'

'Is she now?' Dad looked at Mum over the top of his glasses and she shook her head.

'What's that supposed to mean? I thought you'd be impressed, one of the Hedleys and all that.'

'I'm not impressed by titles and big houses,' Mum blatantly lied. 'Anyway I don't think she is one of the Hedleys.'

'Well she's called Hedley.'

'Being called Hedley and being one of the Hedleys are two completely different things.' She flicked a dishcloth over the surfaces and dropped it in the sink. 'I'm off to my meeting.'

We didn't ask which meeting and I took a second tea-towel and helped Dad finish the drying.

'There's rumours about the people at the Hall,' Dad volunteered. But I didn't want to know and we finished the drying in silence.

I knew there were rumours. I'd heard most of them at school. That the Hall was going to be a hippy commune, a drug den, a centre for polygamy, nothing good. But then no-one in the village ever had anything good to say about anybody, especially not new arrivals. However long we lived in the village and however many committees Mum worked on I knew we'd always be the new people at Verger's Cottage.

It should have been different for the Hedleys, coming back to their roots and all that.

I was still debating which T-shirt I should wear, when Ash banged on the door. He came up to my room and waited whilst I tried on different T-shirts and discarded them in a growing pile on the floor.

'You're worse than a girl, you know,' he said. 'You don't have to make so much effort just for me and Celia.'

'Yeah, well, it's not just you and Celia is it?' I settled on plain black again and re-spiked my hair.

'Not trying to impress the mysterious Angel are you? I'm sick of hearing Celia go on about her. It's "Angel said this," and "Angel thinks that" and, "Angel is sooo interesting."' He mimicked Celia very well and I laughed.

'I've only seen her once but she definitely looks interesting,' I said.

'Yeah? Well, we're about to find out.'

The girls were already at The Plough, sitting on the stone wall outside and waving pint glasses in greeting. Celia was in her usual black. Beside her Angel was a rainbow chick, all pink and silver with a long floaty skirt and a tiny little top which showed off her breasts. Her hair was tied back with a silver scarf, which shimmered down her back like a ripple of water. For probably the first time in my life I was able to describe exactly what a girl was wearing.

It was too hot to sit in the smoky darkness of the bar, so we went out through the pub into the beer garden, where a dozen wooden tables were scattered among the apple trees and overgrown grass. There were a couple of swings and a climbing frame in a corner by the hedge but, thank God, no kids playing on them tonight. The smell of beer, cigarette smoke and flowers mingled in the evening air and the hum of conversation mixed with the late song of bees. We settled ourselves, putting our beer down and pulling chairs up to a table. People from school drifted past our table, stopping to chat.

'Hello Ash mate. David, Celia. See you at the party tomorrow?'

'Last day tomorrow. I cannot wait!'

'Think you've done alright?'

'Michael, do you have to talk about the results tonight? They're not out for ages.' Celia smiled lazily and Michael moved on. Ash glared after him.

'What's he want to talk about the bloody results for?'

'He's only making conversation. Don't be so touchy.'

Ash did seem a bit preoccupied, ignoring half the people who called out to him. Even Celia couldn't get a smile out of him. I shot him a questioning look but he looked away. Sod him, it was Angel I wanted to talk to.

So far she'd sat at the table, quite at ease, sipping her beer and listening to the passing banter. Celia introduced her a couple of times and she responded with a smile but she seemed happy when the chatter stopped and the four of us were left alone.

I was glad Celia was there. Ash had gone silent and all at once I had nothing to say. Angel had this disconcerting way of looking at you, eyes wide and watchful, like she was expecting you to say something fascinating and I didn't want to disappoint her. I kept drinking and smiling, as the girls chatted about school and the village.

'How are you all settling into the Hall?' Celia asked. 'Is there a lot of work to do? It's been empty for so long.'

'Ever since I moved here,' I said.

'For ages longer than that, David. Ten years at least,' Celia corrected.

'It's not too bad, to say it's been neglected for so long,' Angel had a really musical voice. 'But we're just camping in the Hall really, while we get the workshops up and running.' She looked at me from under her heavy eyelids and I took a deep swig of beer. 'Philip wanted to start on the Hall but like Sylvia said we came here to set up an artist's community, not so he could play Lord of the Manor again.'

'Philip? Sylvia?' I enquired.

'My stepdad and my mother. She thinks it makes her sound younger if we call her Sylvia.'

I'd wormed a bit of info about the Hall out of Mum. The Hedleys had been the owners for generations, going back to the 1700s and were earls or barons or something. They had a title anyway. Their main house was in Pimlico but the Hall had been their summer retreat. Over the years the family came to the Hall less and less, until, eventually, about ten years ago they stopped coming altogether. A gardener tried to keep the grounds in order but the house had been left to gently decay. Until now. Philip Hedley was the eldest son of the current Lord and had returned with his wife, her daughter and three kids of their own. And apparently all with the intention of setting up some workshops. I asked Angel to explain.

'We're forming a community for alternative arts. We lived in one in Wales,' she said. 'So when Philip got the Hall from his father we thought we'd try and do it here ourselves.'

'What are alternative arts?' Celia wanted to know. 'Will you be renting out workshops to painters and sculptors and stuff?

'My dad's a painter,' I added conversationally. 'He paints seascapes.'

'Well he won't be painting them with us,' Angel's smile softened her words.

'Why not? David's dad is really good.' Ash suddenly rejoined the conversation and I was touched by his faith in my dad's work.

'I'm sure he is but I doubt he'd want to paint with us. He's not into Pagan art is he David?'

'Pagan art! What on earth is that?' Ash saved me answering. Celia had gone very still.

'Art done by Pagans.'

'But you're not a Pagan are you?' Celia's voice rose and me and Ash stared at her. 'You never said anything about being a Pagan.'

Angel shrugged.

'We're a Pagan community. Is that a problem?'

'I don't know. But I'm a Christian.'

'Yeah and I'm a Pagan. So what? I bet if I'd told you I was a Hindu you wouldn't even have blinked.'

Celia looked embarrassed, 'Probably not. I'm sorry. It just all that sort of thing makes me uncomfortable.'

'Yeah, well so does your Christian stuff but I get over it.' Fortunately Angel was smiling and Celia gave a grudging smile back.

'Well, I don't care what you believe in. I just want to know what you're going to be doing in these workshops. What do Pagan artists make?' I did want to know but I wanted to take the spotlight off Celia. Angel told us that some of the members of the Welsh commune and others they had met on the festival circuit were coming to the Hall. They would paint and sculpt, do complicated things with crystals and runes, make herbal remedies and devise moon blessings. It sounded weird but kind of interesting.

'And do people really believe all that, these days?' Ash sounded sceptical.

'They do, yes.'

'Oh. I'm off for another pint. Anyone else?'

'Not the spiritual type then?' Angel spoke to his retreating back. 'Whereas you David, I reckon you could be.' She turned her gaze on me.

'I've never seen David as spiritual.'

Celia laughed but Angel was serious and said, 'I think David has hidden depths.'

I tried not to look pleased and excused myself to go to the gents. Ash was still at the bar and on the way back I helped him carry the drinks.

'What do think of Angel then?' he asked.

'She's hot!' I burst out, then noticed his expression. 'Well, she seems nice enough. Don't you like her?'

'Not really. All that Pagan crap. Sounds like they're a load of con artists to me. I mean, moon blessings!'

'Well can you at least try to be nice? Celia really likes her.'

'She's not the only one is she? But you know me, always the gentleman. Come on, let's get these drinks to them.'

As the evening wore on and the darkness encroached, Ash was perfectly pleasant to Angel and she responded in kind. When the clock struck the half hour past ten, though, Ash was out of his chair and handing Celia her cardigan before the chimes had faded.

'Time to make a move,' he said and I pushed back my chair to go. A warm hand stopped me.

'You don't have to go as well do you?'

Ash raised his eyebrows but I said, 'No, I guess not.'

'That's good, because if you wait I'll show you where the workshops are going to be.' It clearly wasn't a general invitation so I shrugged apologetically and watched Ash walk away, hand in hand, with Celia.

Chapter Four

I'd wanted to be alone with Angel all night, so why was I so nervous? She leaned back in her chair and lifted her glass, twisting it this way and that to catch the light spilling out from the pub. Together we watched the contents of the glass turn to molten lava.

'So, you've got me alone at last. What do you want to do with me?' Cat's eyes turned on me, glittering in the half light.

I choked on my beer and she laughed, 'You're not that sort of boy.'

I was any kind of boy she wanted me to be. I was finding it hard to swallow. If only I was more like Ash, always knowing what to do, what to say.

'At least you're not like Ashley.'

I laughed but apparently she was serious. 'I know I've only just met him but…' She stopped twirling her glass and looked at me, her head tilted to one side.

'But what?'

'Well, he fancies himself doesn't he? All Mr Ashley hey look at me I'm fantastic-Fitzpatrick. Blokes like him really piss me off.'

I stared at her. 'But he's Ash.' Everybody liked Ash.

'Yeah. And he's your best mate. Sorry. But I can't do with people like that. You know, born with a silver spoon, doting parents, loads of money. Doesn't matter what he does, Daddy will always be there to make it right.' She gave the final word a vicious twist and I looked at her in alarm. We weren't supposed to be fighting but I couldn't let that go.

'Well, he hasn't got doting parents for a start. He never sees his mum, he can't stand her. And his dad won't just hand everything over to him. He has to work in the business you know.'

'Taking German girls sailing on the bay. Tough job! I expect he gets fringe benefits doesn't he?' Her smile was unpleasantly knowing and I looked across the beer garden and saw that almost everyone else had gone. I wished I'd left with the others.

'Ash doesn't cheat on Celia.'

'No? A little saint is he? 'Cos Celia's a Christian isn't she and from what I hear they're not too hot at giving it out.'

'What is wrong with you?' I shoved my chair back and my glass tipped, spilling the dregs across the table. 'We've only just met and all you want to do is have a go at my friends.' I stood up to leave but she jumped up as well and faced me across the now sticky table.

'Don't go. I'm sorry. Don't go. Please.' She reached across the table and caught hold of my arm. Her hand was hot on my skin. 'Stay a bit longer David. I didn't mean it. I didn't, honestly. I say things without thinking.' Her voice was soft and when I looked up her eyes were wide and innocent.

'You can't talk about them like that.'

'Well I can. But I won't if you don't like it. I was wrong. I don't know your friends and I'm sorry.'

'Ok.' I sat down again, this time on Angel's side of the table. The spilt beer dripped onto the grass.

'Do you want another drink?' Her peace offering.

'No. It's fine. I'm going soon.'

'Will you walk me home?' voice almost childlike.

'Well I won't leave you here. Even if you do hate my friends.'

She gave a wry smile. 'I don't hate them. I probably don't like Ash very much. But Celia's lovely. She really is. It's just a shame she's with him.' I opened my mouth and she lifted a pacifying hand. 'Ok it's not a shame. But it's a real shame she's a Christian.'

I didn't know if I was just rising to her bait but I had to ask. Almost wearily I said, 'Why? What's wrong with being a Christian?'

'Like everything. It's so narrow and prejudiced and uptight. It's like signing up to live in a straitjacket.'

'Celia's nothing like that.'

'That's why it's a shame she wants to be a Christian.'

A dozen replies came into my mind. That Celia didn't just want to be a Christian – she was a Christian and it made her happy. That me and Ash didn't mind, so why should Angel? But suddenly I didn't care. I'd had enough arguing for tonight. Angel was weird and opinionated but I still wanted to walk home with her through the cool evening and hopefully she wouldn't talk and things would be fine. She must have read my thoughts.

'Are you ready then? Walk me home in the moonlight.'

Chapter Five

The moon was rising as we left, a silver coin sliding across blue baize, above the church tower.

'Isis,' murmured Angel as she put her hand in mine. When I looked down at our linked fingers I saw that her nail varnish was chipped and she had a small cut above her silver thumb ring. I squeezed her hand and she smiled.

The Hall gates were only a couple of hundred yards from the pub so I walked slowly, savouring every minute. I wondered if I should try to kiss her. Usually girls expected it, a snog and a grope outside the house. I worried what Angel might expect.

The Hall crouched out of sight at the end of an overgrown driveway, guarded by a pair of ornate iron gates. One gate was twisted on its hinges and they both dripped rust flakes into the long grass. Someone had planted a wooden barrel with wild flowers and weeds and the stems straggled onto the gravel, the flowers bleached parchment in the moonlight. I didn't feel welcome but I turned in anyway, only for Angel to pull me back.

'Not that way. Philip's got dogs. They'll bark.'

'And? I don't mind dogs.'

She gave me a withering look. 'No, but everyone'll come out and I'll have to introduce you and crap like that.

And we won't get near the workshops. We're going in the side gate.'

We passed my cottage. The light was burning in the living room and though the curtains were drawn I pictured my parents inside; Mum reading through the minutes of yet another meeting, Dad making a mess of the newspaper or flicking through the channels. And I could be in there too, comfortable, bored, instead of out here, holding hands with an Angel.

Angel had a key to the side gate and wrestled violently with the ancient lock, shaking the gate and cursing until I thought my parents were going to come out and investigate.

'For God's sake give it here.' I held my hand out for the key.

'I can manage. It's just… a bit….stiff. Shit…' she broke away rubbing her hand and I stepped forward and made out that the key turned effortlessly.

'Fine.' Angel pushed past me and through the gate, I followed, rubbing my hand. 'It's a bit overgrown. Nobody comes this way.'

'You don't say.' I tried to avoid adding nettle rash to my injuries as we headed down what might once have been a path but was now a tangle of brambly weeds.

'I nicked the key from Philip's desk the other day. Thought it'd come in useful.'

We made our way through the abandoned shrubbery and across a seeding lawn. A proper path appeared and Angel reached for my hand again. She pressed a finger to her lips and I saw the walls of the house come looming out of the dark. We skirted round and Angel pulled me under a stone archway and into a cobbled courtyard, surrounded by low stone buildings. She swept her hand round in careless ownership.

'Welcome to the Three Ages Centre for the Alternative Arts.' And when I continued to stand and stare around me, 'Well, do you want to see or not?' She ducked into the nearest doorway and I had to follow.

I don't know what I'd expected but I was disappointed. Angel didn't turn the lights on but even the moonlight couldn't disguise that we were looking at some old stables. Tarted up stables but still stables. The walls were painted white and the floors relaid with rough red tiles but the partitions were still in place.

'So the artists have their own space but can feed from each other's artistic flows,' Angel said over her shoulder.

'Right.' I trailed after her into an identical section of white walls and red floors and spaces for artistic flows. I should probably have asked some intelligent questions but they were stables and even Angel wasn't making them seem very exciting.

She pulled me after her through yet another door, 'We're not done yet. This is Sylvia's studio.' She held open a panelled door at the end of the block and followed me in. Sylvia obviously didn't want to share her artistic flows and had a room to herself. She'd spent some time and money on it. The moonlight flowed in through the wide window and spilled onto the polished wood floor. The walls were hung with some billowy material and in one corner was a heap of cushions, all different sizes and textures. There was an easel in front of the window, a tiny desk piled with magazines and a cane bottomed chair.

This is more like it, I thought, as Angel came across the room and kissed me.

She kissed me for a long time and I wrapped my arms around her and kissed her back like I would never stop. I never wanted to stop. I was hard against her leg, only half hoping she wouldn't notice. Then she pulled away and we stood for an age, just looking at each other. The moonlight continued to spill in through the window, my heart continued to beat and she looked right into me, her skin pale, her beautiful mouth a smudge and her eyes glittering darkly.

I wanted her to kiss me again but she didn't. Instead the faint chimes of the church clock and the barking of a dog getting steadily closer propelled her into action and she pushed me out of the room, through the stables and into the darkness.

'Go. Now. Before Philip gets here.' A shove in the back set me running down the path towards the gate. We ran together, gasping for breath as we reached it. She wrenched it open and started to push me through. Then she came after me and caught my hand, pulling me back against her. I smelt incense in her hair as her mouth came close. I bent to kiss her but she turned aside and whispered, 'Meet me here tomorrow afternoon, at three, and I'll show you more than the moonlight.'

And then I was in the lane, the gate between us, and I heard the key rasp shut in the lock.

Chapter Six

I had to tell Ash about Angel. It was the only thing that could have got me out of bed before ten. Mum and Dad had given up calling me in the morning, although Dad did keep muttering about a holiday job. Did he really think I was going to get a job? Especially now?

It was only when I was boiling the kettle and flipping toast that I remembered it was Leaver's Day. How had I forgotten? We'd been arranging it for ages. The plan was, we'd all go down to school one last time, for the buffet the teachers put on, then on to the pub for a couple of hours and finish up going into town. It was going to be great, the last time the whole Year would be together. It was going to be terrible, the last time the whole Year would be together. And I'd managed to forget the whole thing! How was I supposed to meet Angel now? I couldn't miss Leaver's Day, Ash would never forgive me. There was no way I could drop Angel. She'd certainly never forgive me. I'd never forgive myself.

I was so lost in working out how I could be in two places at the same time that I didn't hear the knock on the door until it turned into a hammering.

'Dave. Are you in there? What the fuck are you doing?' It was Ash.

'David. Hi it's us. Are you going to let us in?' And Celia.

I'd been debating how to tell them about me and Angel.

But Ash was no sooner through the door, feet up on the kitchen table before he asked, 'How d'you get on with the mysterious Angel then?'

'Alright. Do you want coffee?' As I spooned granules into three mugs and boiled the kettle again, I found I didn't want to tell him anymore. He'd only take the piss, make out I'd imagined it all.

'Yeah, make it strong. So. Angel?'

'We finished our drinks and we went home. I don't know what you've got against her.' I plonked mugs down, sloshing coffee over Mum's new tablecloth.

'I haven't got anything against her, just don't like all that mystical crap she talks. And she does like to be centre of attention doesn't she? I don't know why Celia likes her so much.'

'She's interesting.' Celia was a bit defensive.

'Very.' They glared at each other across the table.

Celia turned to me, 'Did you see the workshops?'

I thought of denying it. 'Yeah. We only had a quick look 'cos it was dark and I don't think we were supposed to be there.'

'I wouldn't have thought Angel cared what she's supposed to do,' said Ash.

'Anyway they're not finished yet. Just a load of stables really.'

And moonlight, and a beautiful girl and a long, long kiss. Oh, and an invitation to meet her in the afternoon and see more than the moonlight.

We didn't talk about Angel anymore. Instead we reminisced about our school days and how much or little we were going to miss the old place. Celia and I were sad to be leaving, Ash couldn't have been happier.

'I've been wasting my time there these last few years. I'm not one for exams and studying. I want to be out in the world; see exotic places; eat exotic food...'

'Meet exotic women?' put in Celia slyly.

'Never. You're the only girl for me.' And he leaned across the table to meet her lips in a kiss. I looked on with a smile. Usually it bothered me when they messed about. Today it didn't bother me at all. I'd decided I was definitely going to Leavers' Day. I'd invite Angel along as well and we could sneak off later. I excused myself and slipped upstairs to use the phone in my parents' room. It took ages to get the number from directories and by the time the phone was ringing out at the Hall I'd almost changed my mind. Some surly bloke answered and told me Angel was out, he didn't know when she'd be back. I took a risk and left her a message, that I'd see her at The Plough at three o'clock. The bloke grunted and hung up. I debated whether I should phone back until Celia shouted up to me,

'We're going now or we'll be late. You coming?'

Sod it. I ran downstairs.

As ever we walked to school across the fields. We'd trudged this way when the snow topped our shoes and our breaths mingled in front of our faces; and hurried on beautiful spring mornings when wildflowers were thick in the hedges. My favourite times were early in the school year when leaves patchworked our path and there were new books and fresh timetables ahead. Now it was summertime and the sun had come out to salute us. Celia linked arms with us both and we swung along together, matching strides. When we reached the stile I hung back and let the two of them go ahead. Ash held Celia's arm as she scooped up her long skirt to climb the stile. They must have sensed me watching because they both looked up and smiled and I captured the image in my memory like a photograph.

Leavers' Day could have been kind of lame but it wasn't. I got a kick out of calling the teachers by their first names and drinking legitimately on school premises. Ash was bored though. When the speeches and address swapping was over and the whole crowd of us swept out of the school gates, towards the pub, he stretched his arms above his head and gave a contented sigh.

'Well, thank God that's all over,' he said. 'Sorry Celia, but I could not wait to get out of that place. Now my life's my own!'

'To do what?' she asked but I don't think he heard.

We took over the beer garden at The Plough. Derek came out and surveyed his garden, awash with teenagers, beer and wasps.

'Leavers' Day again? Some of you have been coming here for two, three years already. Got held back a year or two did you?' He'd never been big on asking for ID.

'Couple of pints here then we'll piss off away from this lot,' Ash said.

'But everyone's going into town later,' I protested. And Angel's coming to meet me. I'd have to tell him soon.

'Yeah well we can meet them there. But I've had enough of them for now. We can open a bottle at your house or Celia's.'

'Or yours,' said Celia.

'No, not mine. Dad's got a thing I'm drinking too much so best not.' This was news to me. Apart from expecting him to work in the boatyard, Ash's dad never seemed to mind what he did.

Celia nodded though. 'You better be careful with him for a bit. He wasn't impressed after that cock up with the boat trip.'

'What cock up?' I wanted to know but Ash just waved me aside and asked if I wanted beer.

'Yeah, please,' and 'What cock up?' as he walked away.

Celia looked reluctant, 'You know Ash is supposed to help out with the Farne Island trips a couple of times a week?' I did. 'Well he got blasted the other night and he was so hung over he didn't get up to take the trip out. The tour firm threatened to stop using his dad and you can imagine how that went down.'

'Who was Ash drinking with?' It certainly hadn't been me. I'd have reminded him about the trip.

'Some surfer boys he met on the coast. Does it matter?'

It did matter but I let it go and when Ash came back we didn't mention it again.

We were halfway down the second pint when Derek re-emerged from the bar.

'David Wheeler? Is David here?' he yelled, causing a couple of dozen heads to turn in my direction.

I waved, 'Yeah, I'm here. What's up?'

He came across the grass, 'David?' He should've known who I was. He saw me often enough. 'Got a phonecall for you, inside.'

'For me?' I asked as I pushed away from the table. 'Who's ringing me? Here?'

Ash shrugged but Celia looked concerned, 'Maybe your mum or dad need you for something.'

'Like what?' But I ran across the garden and into the narrow hallway behind the bar where the phone was lying on a little table. I looked at it, thinking it was better not to know.

'Go on then.' Derek had followed me in.

'Hello.' There was no reply but I could have sworn I could hear a faint sound, like a sprinkling of bells. 'Hello.' I spoke a bit louder. 'Mum, Dad, is that you?' No reply but the sound of bells grew louder, more insistent. Then a low, feminine laugh.

'Angel? Is that you?' Silence.

'It is you. I can tell. What do you want?' I hoped I sounded confident.

'I thought we had an arrangement David.' Involuntarily I looked at my watch. It was half past three.

'I couldn't make it. It's Leavers' Day and I'm with Ash and Celia. We've had it planned for ages. I left you a message.'

'I didn't get any messages and I'd planned to see you at three.' Yeah well, what did she want me to do? Walk out and leave the others to go on without me?

'It's not too late. If you come now I might be able to forgive you.' Her voice was low and sexy, difficult to resist.

'I can't. I told you. We're going into town. I thought you could come.'

Silence.

'Angel?'

'I'll wait for fifteen minutes but then I'll go and you'll never know what might have happened.' The phone went dead.

I stood and cradled the phone in my hands until Derek came out and took it from me with mutters of, 'need bloody nursemaiding.' I went slowly out into the beer garden, the afternoon sun hot on the back of my neck after the cool of the hallway. Ash saw me and waved his glass, 'Everything alright mate? You ready for another pint.' I shook my head as I approached the table.

'It wasn't bad news was it?' Celia looked concerned and I smiled to say things were fine.

'No, nothing bad. Actually it was Angel.'

'Angel?'

'Angel!' The name burst out of them both at the same time.

'What did she want?' Ash.

'She was reminding me I was supposed meet her this afternoon. At the workshops.'

'Meet her? Today? What for?'

'You didn't tell us?' First Ash, then Celia looked at me incredulously. I didn't have secrets.

'Anyway, you can't,' Ash said flatly.' It's Leavers' Day. I hope you told her.'

'Yeah I did but...'

'But nothing.'

'You're not going are you David?'

It was Celia who nearly broke me down but not quite. Maybe it was time I did have a few secrets.

'Look, I'm sorry but I think I'm going to have to go.' I snatched up my glass, swallowed the warm dregs for some kind of Dutch courage, then started to back away.

'Dave, don't do this mate. That girl is trouble. Celia, tell him he can't piss off like this.'

Celia stayed silent. I gave her one last, apologetic look before I was off, swerving between the tables then breaking into a run.

Chapter Seven

I didn't think at all until I was through the side gate, past the overgrown wood and halfway across the courtyard. Then, something made me stop. This had to be a joke. I halted in the middle of the yard. The sun was beating down on the old cobbles and a dove murmured from the clock tower. It was a perfect day and I was setting myself up for a fall. This was me, David. Not Ash. Not the one the girls fancied. I looked round quickly, half expecting Ash and Celia and the others from school to appear, laughing at me for believing a girl like Angel would want to spend any time with me. I could almost hear Ash's voice, 'Dave, mate. Did you think she was for real? Bet you wished she was.' Clapping me on the shoulder and me laughing along because I hadn't the guts to punch him. Who was I kidding? Ash might not be lurking in the shrubbery but he was sure as hell lurking in my head.

Just then I heard bells again, like on the phone, but louder, more insistent, like water bubbling over pebbles. I looked around. Nothing moved, even the doves had fallen silent. I wondered why there was no work going on in the workshops. Then I saw a door in the corner was ajar. I was sure it had been shut when I looked a moment ago. The sound of bells came again and I started moving towards them. Fuck Ash, fuck the lot of them.

The sunlight spilled after me as I pushed the door open and followed the sound of bells through the stables. I found myself outside Sylvia's room. I put out a tentative hand and the door swung open in front of me. The light behind me met the premature night time of the room and Angel stood on the threshold of the two, framed in darkness.

'You came.'

I nodded but all I could think was that she was wearing a purple robe and I was pretty sure that was all she was wearing.

'Come in then.' She stood aside and I stepped into the room.

'You've been busy.' An understatement. She'd transformed the place. Candles blazed from every surface. The air was heavy with incense, rising from a brass dish in a coil of fragrance. There were cushions everywhere, every shape and size and colour, and vivid coloured throws on the walls and on the floor.

'I've been preparing for you.'

'Right.' I started to laugh but she closed my lips with hers and I was drowning in her and becoming painfully aware that she really did have nothing on under her robe.

She released me and gestured to a pile of cushions.

'Sit down.'

I sank into a velvet embrace.

'Drink.' It was a command rather than an invitation and I held my hand out for the tarnished silver goblet. I drank, thick, honeyed liquid sliding down my throat.

'Nice.'

'It's mead. A sacred drink.'

'Ok.' I drank a bit more. 'Sort of like communion wine?'

'If you like. But better, much better.' And she slid across the cushions until her body was touching mine, from shoulder to hip. She took the goblet from me and laid it aside. 'We can drink again after,' she said.

'After what?' But I never got the words out because she was kissing me again, kissing me like I'd never, ever been kissed, and her hands were under my T-shirt and my hands were pushing the robe from her shoulders.

When I was inside her I opened my eyes and looked down. She looked back, then she smiled and I came in a rush of gratitude and love.

Afterwards, when I looked round for my clothes and started pulling them on, Angel reached out and took my balled T-shirt from me.

'Had enough already? I thought you'd have more stamina.' So I left my clothes and the two of us spent the afternoon naked, drinking mead and I wished Ash could see me now.

When I had to leave she held me close and laid her head against my chest. I wrapped my arms around her and thought what a little, delicate thing she was, how I would do anything to protect her. We parted only when she promised to meet me the next day. And the day after that. And the day after, and ever after.

Chapter Eight

Saturday dawned clear but cool, with fronds of mist still curling in the hedge bottoms. As I opened my bedroom window, Ash drove past in the Land Rover and I waved but he didn't wave back. Probably sulking.

I decided I would walk up to the Hall to meet Angel. That way she might ask me in. She must have read my mind because as I turned in at the gates she was coming out.

'Hi. You're early. I said we'd meet at your house.' She was smiling though.

'Yeah, well, I was up, thought I'd save you the walk.' And when she showed no signs of inviting me back, 'I thought we could go to the coast. I've got a picnic.' I waved a supermarket carrier bag in her general direction.

'Ok. You got a car?'

'No, sorry. I haven't got my licence yet. Well, I've got a provisional but… Anyway I thought we could ride there. Have you got a bike?'

She rolled her eyes and I wished like anything I had Ash's Land Rover, just for one day.

'No but I can nick one from my sister.'

'Sister?'

'Yeah, Sasha, the older one. She's fourteen. Then there's Kenzie, he's twelve and Carmen and - why am I telling you this?' She spread her hands in an expressive shrug.

'The bike?' I ventured.

'Yeah, the bike. God I haven't been on a bike for centuries. Give me five minutes. I'll stick some more food in a bag and I'll meet you back here. Right here.' She pointed at the patch of dried grass at the end of the drive and I wondered if she expected me to sit there and wait for her. She disappeared up the drive, legs long and slim beneath little denim shorts, hair bouncing in a ponytail. I sat down on the grass and waited.

It was a five mile ride to the nearest beach and I wondered if Angel would be OK riding so far if she hadn't been on a bike in centuries. I decided to go slowly and offer lots of breaks. Like she needed that. We covered the distance in record time and it was me craving a break long before we skidded to a gravely halt at the edge of the cliff.

'Slow enough for you?' She grinned and I nodded, trying not to show how out of breath I was. We dumped our bikes behind a clump of hawthorn and made our way down the narrow path to the beach. I loved this strip of coastline. Ash and Celia showed it me the first summer we were friends and we'd had loads of picnics and barbecues in the dunes; gone swimming and got pissed on cheap wine and cider. There were no toilets or cafes selling pop and ice-cream, so hardly anyone came here. I followed Angel down the track, watching her buttocks move under the thin covering of her shorts. She pulled handfuls of cow parsley from along the track and threw them backwards, showering me like confetti.

We found a spot encircled by sand dunes and I spread Dad's old car rug and started unpacking my picnic.

'Beer, cheese, bread – might be a bit stale but I've put plenty of margarine on – a few tomatoes and more beer. OK for you?' I cracked open a beer and leaned back to watch Angel. She knelt on the rug and unfastened a little black rucksack, embroidered with red elephants.

'Wine, wine glasses; only plastic but they'll do; pineapple and cream cheese sandwiches, note the dainty triangle cut; and strawberries, sorry no cream.' She sat back and we looked at her picnic, nicely arranged on paper plates.

'How on earth did you produce that lot in five minutes? You didn't even know we were going on a picnic?' I was a bit fed up. I'd tried really hard.

'Sasha volunteered it. She was messing around doing these fancy sandwiches to impress one of the artist blokes. I told her she was wasting her time and Philip would kill her for nicking a bottle of his wine, so she agreed it would be much better if I took the picnic.'

'I suppose she agreed it would be much better if you had her bike as well?'

'What are big sisters for if they can't stop you making a fool of yourself with older men? Anyway she's only my half sister. Shall I pour?' She passed me a glass of slightly warm wine and a sandwich. I forgot their provenance and raised my glass.

'Cheers,' I said.

'Cheers. Here's to summer.'

'To summer.'

After a while I kissed her and she let me, so I slipped my hand under her T-shirt and discovered she wasn't wearing a bra. So we had sex again and I didn't care if we got caught. Afterwards we lay back on the rug, the sun hot on my chest and legs. I reached out to find a beer but Angel's fingers closed around the bottle first.

'I dare you this, to go swimming in the sea.'

'That's not a dare. I swim off this beach all the time.' I tried to wrestle the bottle from her but she twisted away and stood up, brandishing the beer.

'Go swimming like that – no clothes. And you've got to walk to the sea and back. No running, even if someone sees you.'

'Only if you do.'

'Naturally.' So we joined hands and walked sedately towards the sea. Angel acted like it was no big deal. I wanted to look at her, at her swinging hips and her round breasts but I was struck with shyness and just prayed no-one saw us.

'I didn't know modesty was one of your faults,' Angel said as she paused at the water's edge and did a little twirl, head tipped back and her hair falling all down her bare back.

'It's not,' I said through gritted teeth as I plunged into the water, ignoring the icy shock in my relief at covering up, even though there was no-one in sight.

'Poor little David.' She waded towards me, waist deep in the waves, her breasts sparkling with salt drops. I wanted to lick them off. 'Such a sheltered life he's led.' She put her hands on my shoulders and swung her legs

45

round my waist and we kissed again. 'Not so sheltered now though.'

We were packing up to go before she asked about Ash and Celia. To be honest I hadn't given them a thought. But now she wanted to know when I'd be seeing them again.

'I dunno. Soon I expect.' I didn't really care, they'd be about. They always were.

'But haven't you got stuff arranged for the holidays? I thought you were like Siamese triplets.'

'No. They're just my friends. And yes we've got plans but they can wait. More importantly what are we doing tomorrow?' I tried to put my arm round her but she shrugged me off.

'I don't think you should change everything just because of me.'

What did she mean? She'd already changed everything.

'I mean, you've only just met me and they've been your friends forever, so...'

'I'd rather be with you. I can see them anytime. They won't mind.'

'I was going to say,' and she put a finger across my lips, 'I was going to say I don't mind fitting in with whatever you three have planned.' She stood back and smiled at me expectantly.

'What? You want me to ring you when I'm not with Ash and Celia? See you in between?' I wasn't keen on that idea.

'No I bloody don't!' I thought she was going to stamp her feet. 'I mean I'll come with you, join in, make up a foursome. God you can be thick sometimes.'

'But you don't really like Ash,' I said doubtfully. And the feeling's mutual.

'But you do,' and when I didn't respond, 'So that's sorted then. We can tell them tomorrow.' Just like that.

Ash was going to love it.

Part Two

Lammas

Chapter Nine

I'm sure it was the hottest summer for years. By mid July the sun had come to stay and we forgot that it could ever rain. I loved having Angel around and she more or less fitted in with the others. She tried to wind Ash up sometimes but he refused to bite.

'It's too hot to argue,' he told me when I asked him why he was so mellow. 'And this is the last summer. I'm not letting anything spoil it.'

'Not the last. There'll be loads more summers,' Celia said.

'But the last one like this, the three of us. Before you go away and things change.' I'd never heard him sound wistful before.

We fell back on old habits. We got up late, drank too much coffee and too much beer. We stayed up half the nights and were sick half the mornings. Angel had found a deserted barn and the two of us snuck away to have sex there whenever we got the chance. Life was pretty perfect.

One thing Angel and Celia were never going to agree about was religion. After that first debate at the pub, when Angel announced she was a Pagan, they'd been unable to leave the subject alone. It got quite boring. I mean they were the only two people I knew, under sixty, who had any interest in spiritual things and from what I could see there wasn't much difference between them. I was wrong of course. They both told me so, many, many times. I should have taken my lead from Ash.

'I don't believe in anything, so leave me out of it.' He tolerated Celia going to church but he certainly wasn't going to engage in theological debate. Which was what, it appeared, I was doing one Saturday morning. We were draped all over the front room at the Old Vicarage. Ash had possession of the wingback chair and the sports section of his dad's paper. I was trying to read the main section on the sofa but had Angel wedged at one side of me and Celia curled up at my feet, both banging on about God and expecting me to take sides.

'But don't you both basically believe in the same thing? I mean don't all religions worship the same god really?' I'd heard something like that on the radio and it sounded plausible.

'Don't be bloody stupid.'

'Nooooo!' So they did agree on something then.

'David, Celia's a Christian and I'm a Pagan. How different do you want to get?' Angel said.

'I believe in God and Angel believes in gods,' Celia explained.

'Well, actually you believe in three gods.'

'She's got you there.' Ash looked up from his paper.

'It's still one God, just three different aspects,' Celia said patiently.

'That makes no sense,' Angel shook her head.

I'd always been hazy about the technicalities of church going. There was God, there was Jesus, there was a ghostly thing. You could go on a Sunday and presumably God would wait for you there and you could pray and sing hymns. If I'd wanted to become a Christian I'd have known where to start. But a Pagan? It was a complete blank. I tried saying this but Angel wanted to explain and I really wasn't in the mood.

'Give it a rest Angel. Can we talk about the economy or something really interesting for a change?' Ash dropped the sports section and I stuck out my foot to retrieve it.

'Ok. I'll shut up. But only if you let me show you what I believe in,' Angel said. 'You all have to come to one of my celebrations and see what I do.'

'Alright, but only if you go to church with Celia,' Ash said.

'Hey, I'm not doing some Pagan thing,' Celia looked up, alarmed.

But Angel was already agreeing, 'You're on but you and David have to come as well. This Sunday.'

'It's not entertainment you know. You can't just come to church and watch.' Celia was getting annoyed but Ash and Angel were on a roll. And me? I reckoned I could cope with church for a morning if it meant I got to watch Angel dance naked later on.

Sunday we met in the churchyard just before 10am. It was early for us and I wondered how Celia did it every week. Ash looked shifty, lurking around the grave stones and avoiding the eyes of the regulars who were turning up in twos and threes. Angel was quite at ease, sitting on a flat topped stone, swinging her legs and saying hello to everyone who passed. She seemed oblivious to the looks she was receiving.

'Angel, you shouldn't really sit on the graves,' Celia whispered. Angel shrugged but she did get down and mouthed 'sorry' at Celia as we went into the church. She'd already surprised me by dressing as conservatively as I'd ever seen her, in a long denim skirt and a pink cotton shirt, knotted at the waist so I could see her smooth brown stomach when she moved.

We followed Celia, collecting hymn books and repeating 'good morning' to the woolly grey lady at the back before shuffling into a pew.

'Hasn't fallen down on you yet Angel,' Ash whispered along the pew and Angel grinned back.

'It was you I was worried about.'

Celia silenced them with a glare and we hurriedly got to our feet as the organ sounded the first, deep chord and the vicar began his procession from the back of the church.

It was a Communion service. I hadn't been to one for years and I'd never taken communion. I'd always found there was something disturbing about drinking the blood and eating the body of the person you claimed was your God. The service was actually pretty dull. We stood up and sat down, bowed our heads and faced the altar at various points. I concentrated on keeping my place and mumbled the responses. When the hymns came I mouthed the words, afraid to let Ash and Angel hear me sing out loud. Beside me Celia's responses rung out and her singing voice was sweet and pure. Ash made no attempt to join in but he did stand and sit when prompted. I deliberately avoided catching his eye and was pleased that Angel did the same. In fact she appeared to be taking the whole thing remarkably seriously. It was only when the congregation started shaking hands with everyone and proclaiming 'peace be with you' that she faltered. As I wished I could crawl under the pew to escape, a succession of ladies with blue blazers and neat grey curls approached, proffering papery hands and peace. I saw Angels' lips quiver.

'And peace to YOU.' She bowed over each hand and the ladies soon retreated. When the vicar approached though, she met his gaze with a clear stare and confident smile. He shook hands with all of us and raised his eyebrows to Celia who shrugged.

The prayers and the hymns went on and my attention wandered. I let my eyes roam round the interior of the building, over ancient stone walls and plaques commemorating the worthy parish dead. I wondered what you had to do these days to warrant a big stone plaque. Look after widows and orphans, say the most prayers? Probably leave the biggest legacy. But the building did have atmosphere. Beyond the smells of damp and dust and funeral flowers there was something else, a scent, a whiff of holiness. Like all the prayers ever said and all the psalms ever sung had risen together into the high spaces above us and we were breathing them in, centuries' worth of piety and praise.

I began to feel light headed and was startled by Angel digging me in the ribs and hissing, 'Are you going to take communion?'

I could see a line of people already making their way up to the altar rail and there was a man in a sports jacket at the end of our pew looking at me enquiringly. Celia had already filed out and Angel was following her. Ash remained in his seat.

'If you're not confirmed please go up for a blessing and keep your hands by your side,' the man said. I shook my head at him. He moved on and I wished I had gone up and found out what it was like to be blessed.

Ash leaned across, 'Is it nearly over d'you think? I've had enough.'

'Probably.' I tried to focus on the holy atmosphere again but Ash was restless. He stretched his legs out and yawned. 'Find God then?' he asked.

'Mm.' I concentrated on a stained glass window, on how the sun struck through and set all the tiny coloured panes of glass alight so that the picture of Jesus emerging from the flames, burned with real fire. I closed my eyes and the colours continued to burn inside my eyelids.

'The girls are coming back.'

Did he have to give me a running commentary? I opened my eyes. Angel was striding down the aisle, her eyebrows raised in mock horror. As she pushed past me I smelt wine on her breath.

'Did you take communion? I didn't know you were confirmed,' I said.

'Of course I'm not confirmed. I just wanted to see what

it was like. If I'd be changed.'

'And were you?' Ash asked.

I didn't hear her answer. I was watching Celia. She drifted back towards us, stopping to greet people on each side of the aisle. She was smiling and her face was glowing. She looked as if she had spent the last few minutes with the person she loved most in the world, the person who gave her the most love back. She had always been beautiful to me but for a moment I envied her. She had found something I hadn't known I was missing.

We debriefed under the chestnut tree in the Old Vicarage garden. Ash had invited us over for lunch and as we sprawled on the grass with glasses of white wine, the smell of roasting chicken wafted across the garden. Ash's younger sister Caroline came over and tried to persuade us to pour her a glass of wine.

'You can have one for me Caro but Dad'll flip. He's bad enough about me drinking and I'm 18,' Ash said.

'That's because you get pissed. I only want a glass.'

'Yeah and you're 14. If you have a glass of wine you'll get pissed.'

'Go and get some lemonade and I'll mix you a spritzer.' Celia sat up and reached for the wine bottle.

'Saint Celia, always has the answer,' Angel said from behind her shades.

Celia laughed, 'I wish. Anyway, from saint to sinners, what did you think of church this morning?'

'Yeah, what did you think?' Caro rejoined us. 'Dad nearly fell off his chair when I said Ash had gone to church.

Said he thought the only way we'd get him in there would be in a box.'

'Nice,' said Ash. 'I'd go to church to marry Celia.' He squeezed her thigh and she blushed.

'Church was exactly what I expected,' Angel was lying on her back, hands crossed behind her head, staring straight up into the branches of the tree. 'It was dull, bland and safe.'

'I wouldn't go that far,' said Ash, though I knew dull was exactly what he thought.

Celia hugged her knees and looked at me. 'OK. What did you think David?'

Angel rolled over and pushed her shades off her face to look at me.

'I thought it was OK.'

'Just OK?' Celia sounded disappointed

'You looked like you were getting right into it to me,' Ash said. 'You had your eyes shut and everything.'

'Oh yeah,' Celia and Angel said at the same time but the inflections were so different.

'Well, I was giving it a go. Getting the atmosphere. But I don't think we do get it. Not like Celia. To us it's just words but to her it's real.' I was picturing Celia as she walked back from communion. It wasn't something I could explain.

'Real but dull.' Angel pushed her shades over her eyes again.

'Well, it's your turn now.' Celia didn't seem too put out. 'You've got to show us how Pagans do it. And we'll expect excitement.'

'You sure you're up for it? Isn't it against the rules for Christians to go Pagan?'

'I think God'll let me off this once. So what will it be?'

'We'll celebrate Lammas. On the 1st August.'

Ash's dad called us for lunch then and we left religion lying with the wineglasses, under the chestnut tree.

Chapter Ten

We celebrated Lammas in the evening, as the sun was beginning his slow descent into darkness. The heat hardly lessened as the light faded and my T-shirt was soaked in sweat long before we reached the place Angel had chosen. She'd loaded me like a packhorse, whilst she skipped lightly through hedge shadows. Celia walked hand in hand with Ash but barely replied when I spoke to her.

About a mile from the village there was an ancient tower, relic of the days of the Border Reivers. At weekends it opened to the public and the grassy car park became a puzzle of picnics and pushchairs but in the evenings the tower stood solitary, circled by its swathe of mown grass. Angel climbed the gate at the entrance and signalled we should follow her. She settled on the grass beneath the tower walls and spread out her skirt in a crimson semicircle. She looked up expectantly and we arranged ourselves around her. I handed her the rucksack and she emptied the contents onto the grass

'Now normally we wouldn't have eats or drinks till we'd finished but this isn't going to be a full on Pagan ceremony – with having a Christian among us.' She nodded towards Celia who nodded back. 'So we'll have a drink to start us off. This is supposed to be fun.' She looked round at us. 'It's not church.'

Celia didn't rise to the bait and Angel handed wooden goblets round, then filled them with mead. Her eyes met mine across the top of her cup, 'David is very fond of mead. He sampled it and me for the first time on the same afternoon. A very hot afternoon I seem to remember!' she giggled. I pretended to be embarrassed but shot Ash a sideways glance and was gratified to see he looked pissed off.

'I've brought seed cake as well but we'll save that for later.' She lay back, folded her arms behind her head and stared up at the darkening sky. Unsure, the rest of us sipped our mead and looked at each other.

'Are we going to do anything else or is this it?' Ash asked eventually.' I mean I'm never one to knock sitting about having a drink but I'd prefer a pint down The Plough.'

Angel sat up abruptly. 'I was trying to focus myself but we might as well get on with it. Now, do you have any idea what Lammas is about?'

'It's a festival of first fruits, celebrated by Christians for centuries and it used to be one of the big hiring fairs,' Celia said. Angel looked a bit taken aback.

'It might have been hijacked by the Christians but it's not a Christian festival! It is to celebrate the first fruits of the harvest but also,' and she shot a sharp look at Celia, 'to commemorate the Sun God who lays down his life tonight for the sake of the harvest. And that's definitely not Christian!'

A God who laid down his life for others sounded vaguely familiar and Celia's lip curled in a knowing smile, though she didn't say a word.

Angel told us lots of things about Lammas – a pregnant goddess, the lord of the harvest, somebody called Mary Barleycorn and I tried to pay attention whilst thinking how good she looked in red.

'... the God and Goddess lie together for the last time.' She had my attention now. 'The last time before the God sacrifices himself and lets his power flow back into the earth. Sometimes we re-enact their final farewell, but I thought perhaps not tonight. Or maybe we could do that later.'

I hadn't time to turn scarlet or to really see how Celia and Ash took that before Angel was on her feet and dragging us along with her. She demanded we join hands and then started to walk us round in a circle, clockwise. Celia was pale and her lips set in a tight line.

'First we go deosil, that's clockwise, to raise the power in the circle. She pulled us round faster and faster, and I struggled to keep my balance. 'And we summon the power of the Guardians of the four winds.' She raised her face skywards as she circled and chanted to the Guardian Spirits of the North and the South, the East and the West. I barely recognised her and it felt like we were intruding into her sacred world. I avoided looking at the other two. I couldn't stand for Ash to laugh at her.

Then, abruptly she stopped the circling and we sat round whilst she lit incense and an orange candle and sprinkled salt in a circle. She produced a corn dolly, 'Mary

Barleycorn and the symbol of the Goddess,' she said, then passed the figure through the incense smoke and the flame, before handing her on to each of us. 'Make your promise to the Goddess.'

Celia passed her on as if the little doll were on fire. Ash ran his hands slowly over the figure and met Angel's eyes with a long, suggestive gaze. I snatched Mary from him and glared and Angel laughed at us both. It didn't feel very holy.

Then she uncorked the bottle of mead and poured some into the centre of the circle, chanting,

'Dark lord melts into the night

Taking with him summer's light.

Merging wishes, law and might

Removing evil from our sight.

This is our libation, poured in memory of the God, in love of the Goddess, in thanks for the harvest. Blessed be.' And it all seemed to be over.

Angel cut the seed cake and Ash poured more mead, before, as he put it, Angel could waste any more on the soil. I was about to ask Celia how she'd found it but Angel put a hand up to stop me.

'The ritual is over. But now we have to learn the lesson for the season. We have to assess our harvest, what we've achieved in the year, what we've learned and what we can change. Shall I go first?' No-one argued. 'I've left everything I loved in Wales but found I didn't need it anyway. I've learned that I never want to stay in one place for more than one turn of the year and that you have to make your life into what you want it to be. You take your harvest where you find it and if it's someone else's first then maybe they just didn't appreciate it. Get the idea?'

'I get it just fine,' Celia sat up and hugged her knees. 'I'll go next shall I? This year I've learned you have to work hard for what you want, that my faith means everything to me and that when you find love you have to hold onto it, because there is nothing more precious and nothing more worth fighting for.'

'How romantic,' said Angel.

'Only if the truth is romantic. Go on David, tell us about your harvest.'

I had no idea what was simmering between Angel and Celia but the static was practically crackling. I had no idea either what my harvest was so I blurted out the things that were most in my thoughts, 'I've found love and Celia's right. It is the most precious thing.' I tried to meet Angel's eye but she was staring into her goblet. 'And I've found sex and that's pretty precious too!'

God knows why I said that. When I told Ash it was his turn he said, 'I'm not talking some crap about my personal harvest. And I think we could have done without hearing about yours. If we've finished here I'm off to the pub.' He hauled Celia to her feet and they set off, leaving Angel and me to clear up the cups and candles. As we placed everything back into the rucksack Angel reached over and kissed me on the lips.

'I think that went rather well, don't you?'

Chapter Eleven

Conflict was inevitable. If just two Pagan artists with alternative clothing, painting and ideas had moved into the village there would have been ripples. Make that twenty and you're talking tidal wave. Angel buzzed with excitement as the Hall filled with her hippy friends from Wales and I'd never seen her so happy or so high.

The village buzzed too. Because I was usually with Angel, I missed out on most of the gossip. But not my parents. Mum was a member of every social group and committee within fifty miles and even Dad was secretary of the cricket club and drank regularly in that hub of gossip, The Plough.

The problem wasn't that the artists had moved into the Hall, it was that no-one knew what they were doing there and didn't seem likely to find out. If Angel was anything to go by invitations to visit were not going to be flying around.

'So,' my mother told us over an unseasonal shepherd's pie, 'we've decided that we should invite Lady Hedley to join the Needlework Guild and the Coffee for Good Causes Circle. She's probably waiting for a chance to enter into village life and is just too shy.'

Dad and I exchanged glances.

'I don't think Angel's mum is shy,' I said.

'Do Ladies of the realm join Coffee Circles?' Dad wanted to know. 'You should probably invite her to be patron.'

'I should think she'll be quite happy to be a member like everyone else,' Mum snapped and a couple of days later the invitation was despatched.

Angel had told me and Celia a while ago that the Reverend Armstrong had already been to the Hall to make his welcoming pastoral visit.

'He turned up with a copy of the parish magazine and a list of service times. You can imagine how that went down. I mean we are Pagans!'

'He probably didn't know that,' Celia said.

'When he saw you in church with us the other day, I bet he thought he had a convert,' I laughed.

'Don't!' said Angel with a real shudder. 'I think we scared him off though. Philip told him we had no time for his superstitious nonsense but nonetheless would he like to take tea with Lady Hedley. So Sylvia greeted him in the drawing room in her caftan and turban and gave him nettle and blackberry tea, while she told him all about the community's principles, in case he ever felt the need for a change.' Angel doubled up laughing and even Celia grinned.

In the meantime Philip Hedley was endearing himself to his neighbours by refusing to maintain his boundaries. When he'd been an absentee landlord the local farmers kept the hedges and fences secure. Now he was in residence they expected him to do his share. Which he wasn't prepared to do. He announced his reasons to a surprised farmer, who dared to enquire when Philip was going to repair the hedge on New Meadow.

'I don't intend to mend the hedge at New Meadow, Old Meadow or any other meadow. I don't believe that land should be parcelled up and anyway I like to see animals roaming free. Don't worry if a few sheep come over to my side. We're mostly vegetarians so they won't come to any harm.'

It might have been coincidence or design which brought both my parents home on the same evening, bursting with the iniquities of 'those Hedley's.' Against Dad's advice the cricket club had asked Philip to resume his family's traditional position as president of the cricket club and invited him to deliver the speech at the annual dinner. The reply arrived the same day that Sylvia Hedley responded to her invitations to join the Coffee Circle and Needlecraft Guild.

I was sitting at the kitchen table reading the paper and waiting for Ash to come round, when Dad came in, looking uncharacteristically cross.

'That Hedley claims he's a man of the people but he's as stuck up and conceited as any of the so called aristocracy.'

'Oh?' I raised my eyebrows. 'I didn't know you had a problem with the aristocracy.'

'I don't. I don't know any of them. I don't know this Hedley mind, but...'

'That woman! I told you they were no good. Didn't I tell you?' and Mum marched into the kitchen and slammed a tangle of needlework and papers on the table. I quietly withdrew my newspaper and folded it up.

'Dad was just telling me about Philip Hedley,' I said.

'Philip Hedley? Never mind him. It's her I'm concerned with. Put the kettle on Eric.' Dad moved to the kettle. His story would have to wait.

'Her Ladyship has kindly replied to our very friendly invitation to join our groups.'

'I take it she wasn't keen then?' Dad said.

'No, not keen at all. In fact she said, and I quote, *Thank you for your invitation to join your little coffee and sewing societies. I must decline. Not only am I far too busy establishing our community of thinkers and artists but I doubt I would be able to satisfy your desire for gossip about our lives and work. Sylvia Hedley.* Have you ever heard anything like it! Gossip! As if we care two figs about her stupid community and what they get up to. Although some of the stories I've heard today…'

'Dad. What were you saying about Philip Hedley?' I stalled her.

'They must have caught the letter writing bug up at the Hall. We sent our invitation out and back it came and on the reverse he's written…' Dad produced said invitation from his pocket.

'*….not only do I dislike cricket but I disapprove most strongly of honorary titles and positions. Whilst I was keen to return to my family home it was with a view to founding a new kind of community, similar to the one I knew in Wales. I have* *no intention of taking up the old positions and customs of my family...* The patronising so and so. I didn't want him at our dinner anyway.'

'Quite right Eric. Have we any biscuits?'

I left them to their competitive outrage and went upstairs to wait for Ash, and to think about my own member of the Hedley family, who, I was fairly confident, had a hand in both the letters.

Chapter Twelve

When I'd just about given up hoping for an invitation to meet any of the Hedleys, I bumped into the Lord himself, coming out of the village shop. I didn't know it was him at the time or I would have introduced myself. I still had visions of tea in the drawing room with little cakes arranged on a fancy stand and a butler who called me sir.

China teacups and butlers didn't spring readily to mind when I stood aside to let a thin bloke, with a thin grey ponytail and bare feet, out of the narrow shop doorway. Joints and squats maybe. He wandered out of the shop with a carton of fags and a bottle under his arm and nodded vaguely at me. I went into the shop and Jilly, the assistant greeted me.

'What do you think of the new Lord Hedley then?'

I told her I didn't know, I hadn't met him.

'You just passed him, leaving the shop.'

I stared. 'Are you sure?'

'Oh yeah. He comes in every week, buying cigarettes and whisky. He's quite friendly but not what you'd expect is he? Think he'd have a bit more class.'

I nodded. I was disappointed. I knew Angel's family were meant to be Bohemians, I mean look at Angel. But she glowed and sparkled and this bloke was just...well he was grubby.

Obviously I didn't comment on her stepfather's lack of personal hygiene when I next saw Angel. We were lying on the straw in the barn and I was running my fingers up and down her inner thigh. 'I met your stepdad yesterday.'

She pushed my hand away and sat up, 'Where? You haven't been up to the Hall have you?'

'No. I saw him in the shop. But would it be such a crime if I did go to the Hall? It's not like you're ever going to invite me is it?

'No I'm bloody not. Did you speak to him?'

I admitted I hadn't actually known it was him at the time and she relaxed.

'Why don't you want me to meet your family anyway? They can't be that bad.' I moved round behind her and started massaging her shoulders.

'Philip's not my family. Not really. Sylvia married him, that's all. She could have married anyone. That's the thing with families. You're stuck with them because of who you're born, not who you are. If you met my family you'd think I was one of them and I'm not. I'm nothing like them. I'm nothing like anyone.' She put her arms around my neck and I kissed her. Soon we were entwined in the straw again. But afterwards I asked her, 'How did your mum come to marry Philip Hedley? I know he's not your average Peer of the Realm but he's still got a title and land and all that.'

'And I'm just a common little tart from Wales you mean?' But she was laughing. 'If I tell you one story about

71

how Sylvia and Philip met will you shut up about my family?'

I promised and she propped her chin on her hands and told me, 'My dad was guitarist in a band and Sylvia was a groupie, so you can guess how long that relationship lasted. He knocked her up then he went on tour and left her behind. She was seventeen and decided she'd go after him. I don't know if she ever found him. If she did it didn't come to anything. I've never met him.' A flash of bitterness.

'Anyway she found she liked life on the road – festivals all summer and somewhere warm to hibernate in winter. Which is how I came to be born in a Manchester squat, in the middle of December, with Sylvia's teenage friend playing emergency midwife. Have you got any fags?'

I reminded her I didn't smoke.

'What am I doing with such a good boy?' she shook her head. 'We went back on the road soon as winter ended and that's what I remember, long summers in the van, camping in fields without permission and pissing the locals off. Then winters in some horrible town or back with Sylvia's parents when her money ran out. And don't ask me about them 'cos I won't tell you.'

'And when did she meet Philip?'

'I was coming to that. While Sylvia was doing her New Age pilgrimages, with daughter in tow, the Honourable Philip Hedley was growing up in Pimlico or Chelsea or somewhere with all of life's little benefits. You know posh school, pony club, cousins called Tristan. God I need a fag.'

I still didn't smoke and in a bit she carried on.

'I don't know why you want to know all this. Anyway, his daddy wanted him to join the family firm and become a banker. He's a born banker if you ask me. But Philip wanted to be a potter instead and enrolled at the local college. His mummy thought that was a terrible idea, just think of all the common people he might meet. So she bought him a wheel and a kiln so he could play at making pots at home. But it didn't work 'cos Philip donated his wheel and his kiln to the college and went there to use them.' Angel sat up abruptly and started looking round for her clothes.

'Don't stop there. How did Philip meet Sylvia? And what were they doing in a commune in Wales and why did Philip come back here?'

Angel was pulling her T-shirt over head and reaching for her shorts, 'Nah, that's your lot. I've had enough. I'm off to buy some fags.'

Chapter Thirteen

I hadn't seen Ash and Celia since Lammas. Then Ash rang and asked if me and Angel wanted to go on one of his seal trips. A couple of times a week he took a boat out to the seal colony on the Farne Islands, for his dad. In previous summers me and Celia had gone along whenever he had spare seats. Now a family party had cancelled and there was room for us all.

'Do I really want to go and look at seals with a load of cooing tourists?' Angel drawled.

'Yes,' I said firmly and she gave in with a sigh.

There were about fifteen of us, a mixture of young couples, families and pensioners with pac-a-macs and sandwiches. Ash met them all with a smile, helped them into the boat and pushed off from the quay with a smooth, confident movement. I was always amazed how my sarcastic, moody friend, usually too cool to be enthusiastic, could morph into Ash the professional tour guide. Apart from a brief 'hi' and a wave he hardly acknowledged us but Celia never took her eyes off him. Angel dug me in the ribs.

'Fancies himself doesn't he?' she nodded towards Ash, standing in the stern of the boat, one hand on the tiller. 'Sadly he has the looks to get away with it.'

I stared as she flicked her hair off her face and settled her shades over her eyes.

I knew Ash's commentary practically by heart. Still he did deliver it very well.'You'll see along the wall of the cliff the nesting sites of all these birds flying around us now. This is one of the quieter times of year for the colonies as the fledglings have left the nest but in the mating season these cliffs are full of the male birds showing off their plumage and their acrobatic skills to impress the females.' The birds wheeled around us in their thousands, the air reeling with harsh calls. In my case it was the plumage of the female which attracted. I squeezed her waist and she wriggled away.

We must have seen the seals a dozen times but as we neared the rocks where they sunned themselves in plump abandon Celia sat up and I nudged Angel.

'Look. Seals.'

She didn't remove her shades but she did look over. 'Seals indeed. And rather a lot of them.'

Ash finished his commentary and held the boat close in to shore so everyone could stare at the sad eyed seals. He turned his mike off to talk to us.

'I heard yesterday that the colony's going to be culled in the next couple of seasons 'cos it's getting too big for the area to sustain. It happened a couple of years ago when there wasn't enough food to keep the colony going and seals were dying and rotting on the rocks, spreading disease.'

'What will they do? Shoot them?' I asked.

'Yeah probably the quickest way.'

'But those poor seals,' Celia looked really upset. 'Can't they move them or bring in extra food or something?'

'I think they should just leave them.' This from Angel.

'But they can't. That's what I just said. If they do they'll start starving to death.'

'Then they would starve. A natural cull. Why does man have to get involved?'

'Because it's barbaric to let animals starve to death. It's even worse than shooting them, which I don't think they should do anyway,' Celia was leaning forward, her voice low so the passengers wouldn't hear her.

'Nature is barbaric. It's the way life is. Survival of the fittest. Winner takes all. You can't just get involved when it suits, to pretty things up. I say let them die.' Angel moved out of the circle of my arm.

'Do you really believe that?' Celia asked. 'Let nature sort it out, however brutal?'

'I really do.' Angel tilted her face towards the sun.

After the seal trip things changed. I had no idea why but I'd clearly done something right. Because Angel fell in love with me, openly, demonstratively, wonderfully. Before, she'd talked about sex in front of the others like it was a badge of honour, to embarrass me and to shock the others. But when I tried to show how I felt, an arm round her waist, a sneaked kiss just in Ash's eyeline she pushed me away, whispered 'Not now.' All that changed. She couldn't keep her hands off me. She held my hand – all the time, kissed the back of my neck and ran her fingers up and down the inside of my arm. She draped herself across my lap and stroked my thigh as we sat together. If anything she was most affectionate when Ash and Celia were around. And it was pissing them off.

I didn't care. I'd had to put up with the two of them kissing and whispering for years. It was my turn now. Except I was one step ahead of Ash. I was shagging Angel, whilst him and Celia, well, it never went that far did it?

So when I noticed Ash was moodier than usual and drinking more, I ignored it. When Celia seemed to withdraw into herself and have less and less to say, I left her alone. They were just jealous weren't they? I'd been jealous for years.

One Wednesday, about a week before the A level results came out, Ash asked if I wanted to go over to Seahouses, to pick up a boat for his dad.

'Just the two of us. Have lunch at The Ship on the way.'

'What about the girls?'

'Sod the girls. It's ages since we did anything without them. You're not actually glued to Angel are you? I mean, you can operate without her?'

Stung, I said of course I could and we took the Land Rover and the trailer and drove erratically down the coast, with the radio on full blast. The windscreen was peppered with flies and dust churned up from the wheels so we progressed in an amber haze. I trailed my arm out of the window and we both sang too loudly. I'd missed Ash, even though he'd been there all summer.

At The Ship we ordered sandwiches and beer and sat outside, looking along the coast. In the distance Bamburgh Castle basked in the heat, impregnable and untroubled against the blue sky. I watched the seagulls circling in the blue above us. I was in a sun-soaked daze, content to linger over my lunch, to talk about nothing as the day wore on. Ash was not.

He crashed into my thoughts, 'Do you know what's up with Celia?'

'What?' I looked at him, bemused. Celia was miles from my thoughts.

'I said, do you know what's up with Celia?'

'Why? Is she poorly or something?'

'Of course not. I mean do you know why she's so miserable all the time?' He pushed his hand through his hair.

'I didn't know she was. She has been a bit quiet lately,' I conceded, 'but then you haven't exactly been sweetness and light have you? I thought you'd had a row or something.' I took a bite of my cheese and onion roll.

'Me and Celia don't have rows. And there's nothing wrong with me,' he glared. 'I should have known you hadn't noticed. Used to be you'd react if Celia blinked more than usual. But I guess you've moved on.'

That was unfair. I'd tried for years not to care too much about Celia, to please him. Now, apparently, I didn't care enough. I took a couple of deep gulps of my beer and watched a gull skimming the wave tips before I turned back. Ash was rolling his glass between his palms and frowning, his fringe falling in his eyes again. I wanted to brush it aside.

'I told you, I think she's been a bit quiet lately. She might just be worrying about the results,' I said.

He looked up. 'Not Celia. She might not say it but she knows she's walked those exams. It's just a question of how many A grades she gets. No, I think it's to do with God.' And he looked away, embarrassed. I wasn't surprised.

'Yeah, right. D'you want another pint?' If we were going to talk about God I'd need one.

So he told me what I should already have known. That Celia had stopped going to church. That she wouldn't say why. That she got angry if he asked her. Told him she had other things in her life than church, was more than just a Christian, had other things to talk about than God.

'It wasn't like I was having a go at her either. I was just asking if I should meet her after church. But she went right off at me. You should ask Angel.'

'Angel was there?'

'Yeah. I can't remember why. She was all concerned, asked Celia if everything was alright. Was quite nice really.' Grudgingly conceded. 'She only made it worse. Celia told us to fuck off and went home.'

'Celia told you to fuck off? That's a first,' I grinned.

'I was quite hurt,' he said seriously, then he caught my eye and we started to laugh.

Chapter Fourteen

All summer, results day had been the cloud on my horizon, the day when plans and ambitions could be screwed up and tossed into life's rubbish bin. I'd worked hard enough. I mean you can always put in a few more hours study, have one less night with your mates, do one more past paper but I had tried. I wanted university life badly. I needed to get back to the city, to feel the streets close round me with all the urban clutter and possibilities. I wanted to drink too much and sleep too little, sit round and smoke dope in poky little rooms, watch new bands in back street pubs and walk home in foggy dawns.

Ash and Celia had always been part of the plan. We were all going to study in the city. Now I fitted Angel into the picture. I could already see her in my student flat, stretched out on the bed with a bottle of wine and a spliff, not having to play at being Bohemian. With Angel to visit me every weekend I'd have instant credibility. Except now my pretty dreams might be ripped up and I'd be condemned to some dull course at some dismal college because I hadn't got the right grades.

It didn't seem right, walking across the fields to school again. I'd finished with all that. I felt a million years older and wiser than the David who'd sat his exams here. We could have waited a day and had the results delivered in the post. But who was going to do that?

We walked in silence this time. Celia was white with nerves, needlessly I thought. Ash acted like it was nothing to him, hands in his pockets, whistling tunelessly and kicking a stone in front of him. He had more cause to be worried. I knew how many nights he'd spent down the pub and how many Saturdays out on the bay. I don't think Celia realised just how little he'd studied. When she was tucked up in her cottage with her books she fondly trusted Ash was doing the same. I didn't know which one I'd been protecting.

The results were pinned on a notice board outside the main office. There was already a cluster of students, anxiously scanning the lists. It was an unwritten rule that no-one would announce anyone else's results but as we pushed our way through a couple of people smiled at me and a core of confidence started to glow inside. I saw someone reach out and squeeze Celia's arm. She was alright then. It seemed though, that no-one was meeting Ash's eye.

It took about ten seconds to find my name at the bottom of the list and another three to read the results – Wilson, David : Economics B; English A; General Studies C; Geography B. I suppressed a shriek of exultation. I was in! I'd done it! For those few moments nothing and no-one else mattered. When I found Lambert, Celia Jayne: Art

A; English A; General Studies B; History A, my jubilation increased and I turned to hug Celia. She didn't hug me back and I followed her gaze. Fitzpatrick, Ashley James: French E; Geography F; History F.'Shit, Ash.' I turned but he was already gone.

I suppose we should have followed him straight away but it was hard to ignore the congratulations, not to congratulate others in turn, ask what they'd got and bask in Celia's reflected glory. She'd got the top marks in the year. I knew how pleased she was but she wouldn't let it show.

'It doesn't matter what I got. What's Ash going to do?'

I didn't know. I didn't care as much as she did and I let her run after him, watching her long skirts flapping as she caught up with him halfway across the school field. I saw her take hold of his arm and him fling her hand off and march on. She reached out again and he swung round and I thought, for a second, he was going to hit her. But she held out her arms and he let her hold him. They stood there for ages, backlit by the sun. I watched them until they broke apart and joined hands to walk away across the fields. I turned back to the celebrations but in my head I could still see Ash's head falling onto Celia's shoulders, see her arms enfold him as if she could protect him from himself.

Chapter Fifteen

Angel might have been enjoying the friction between the village and the Hall but Philip was having second thoughts. He unexpectedly announced he was throwing open the workshops one Saturday and everyone was welcome to come and see the artists' work. Angel decided he'd arranged it purely to piss her off.

'An Open Day! I mean, a bloody Open Day and Sylvia's letting him! She won't be there but she's still letting him do it!'

'What about the auras?' I asked.

'Exactly! It's going the ruin the atmosphere. A load of bloody nosy villagers poking about and laughing and calling us hippies. What the hell is he playing at!'

I'd never seen her so agitated. Personally I thought it was a great idea. If I wasn't going to get any more personal tours of the place, this was the next best thing.

Ash and Celia didn't agree. Celia told me flatly she wasn't going and when I asked her why she said, 'Because I don't want to.'

Ash was equally reluctant. Even the promise of a bar wasn't enough to tempt him out of his post results lethargy. I resigned myself to going on my own and told Angel she'd have two less non-believers messing up the auras. I thought she'd be pleased. Instead she was inexplicably annoyed and insisted on us going over to Celia's house, just so she could invite her mum.

"Cos if she comes, Celia'll come and if Celia comes, so will Ash.' I didn't bother asking why she was so concerned whether they came or not.

I was definitely not going to the Open Day with my mum and dad. Mum was disappointed. I think she was secretly hoping for introductions and a personal tour. Some hope. Did Angel's family even know I existed?

Having got rid of my parents, who were going to 'wander along later,' I wasn't happy to be landed with Celia's mum. She was alright but I didn't think she'd get the point of wind painting or aura healing. I didn't really get the point either but at least I thought there was a point. As expected, Mrs Lambert was overdressed and enthusiastic. Celia was annoyed with her mother and Ash was in a sulk with Celia. I wished I'd gone on my own.

Cars had been banned and we joined a trickle of villagers and strangers, already marching up the driveway to the Hall. A thin plume of dust wavered in our wake.

I'd only ever caught glimpses of the Hall before, of sharply angled roofs and darkly glittering leaded windows. Now I tried not to show how impressed I was. The place was huge. Turreted towers guarded each end and huge bays rose up three storeys in an expanse of leaded glass and ornate stone sills. It was a house which made me think of Huntsmen's balls and carriages at dawn, Angel in a sweeping gown sipping champagne with me on the terrace. Then I realised that the house was decaying where it stood and its days of grandeur were as far away from reality as Angel in a ballgown.

As we crossed a lawn thick with daisies, I tried to see through the windows. The glass was opaque with dust and dirty drapes hung across inside.

Celia's mum came up beside me. 'Must be very dark. I bet the rooms are lovely though, aren't they?'

'Mm.'

'You'd think they'd have made a bit more of an effort though, with all these people coming.' Mrs Lambert turned to Celia, who shrugged. 'They could at least have mown the lawn and cleaned the windows. It looks so neglected.'

Privately I agreed with her. I'd hoped for some sign that this was a house of artists – weird garden sculptures or rainbow murals glimpsed through the window. But I had to stick up for Angel. 'They've only been here a couple of months and they've concentrated on the workshops. They'll do the house later.' Remembering Philip Hedley drifting out of the village shop, I had my doubts.

'If this was my house it wouldn't look so sad,' Celia's mum was adamant, 'Two months and not so much as a flower to welcome a visitor.'

'Plenty of flowers on the lawn Mrs L,' Ash pointed to the blossoming weeds pushing up around our feet. Mrs Lambert smiled and we moved on, following a series of paper arrows, through a small stone archway onto the narrow path to the stables.

As we proceeded in convoy, Mrs Lambert leading the way, there was a flash of silver and blue and Angel appeared in front of us, wearing a floor length skirt and a fantastic scowl. Celia shrank back beside me as Angel blocked our way. She was pale and her eyes dark circled as if she hadn't slept in nights. 'You all came then? Couldn't resist a chance to see the hippies at play and have a good laugh at us? Well you are all most welcome.' She swept a deep curtsy in front of us.

'But you invited us Angel, dear,' Mrs Lambert was at a loss and I wondered if Angel had been drinking.

'Ignore her.' Celia took her mum's arm and steered her round Angel. 'I think it's this way.'

Angel stepped aside to let them pass and Ash hurried after them with a sidelong grin at Angel.

'You going with them?' She spun round to face me, eyebrows still drawn in a fierce line across her forehead.

'Do you want me to?' I reached for her hand, unrolling the clenched fingers and then she started to laugh, the sudden change like sunlight chasing shadows across a hillside. Her eyes cleared and sparkled and I was laughing with her.

'Come on then. Let's go and join the show,' she said.

The familiar courtyard was unfamiliarly busy and the doves had taken flight. Instead there were visitors flocking in the corners and doorways, chattering like sparrows. Some of them had plastic cups in their hands, others clutched oddly shaped packages. I recognised a few faces from the village but Ash and Celia were nowhere to be seen. Something of Angel's anger flickered in me. These

86

people were in the way, cluttering the space with their chatter and their curiosity.

Angel looked round with curled lip, 'As you're here I might as well show you round. At least I can trust you not to laugh. Even if you haven't got a clue what we're really doing.'

'That's not true.' I'd tried really hard to get into all her spiritual art stuff. She ignored me.

'I thought you might want to have another look at my mother's studio. Obviously it's not open to the public today, but I do have a key.' She dangled a key on a length of ribbon in front of me. 'Maybe we could relive our very first time.' She whispered these last words right into my ear, then ran her tongue around the lobe and down the side of my throat.

'Bloody hell Angel,' I jolted away from her, as if I'd had an electric shock. 'Not here. My mum and dad'll be here any minute.'

'Where then?' She sidled close again and slid her fingers under the waistband of my jeans.

'Is my stepdaughter corrupting you?' Lord Hedley appeared in a smock and cut off denims. 'Never mind her, have some punch. About 40% proof. Help you cope with anything. Even my stepdaughter.' He thrust a plastic glass of something pink into my hand, tapped Angel affectionately on the shoulder and passed on, villagers moving carefully out of his way as he went.

'Tosser. Why he wanted to invite all these people I do not know. Sylvia's got the right idea. She's locked herself in the attic with a bottle of champagne until it's over.'

'So why did he invite everyone?' I asked as we started to negotiate our way across the courtyard. I had a sip of the punch. It had a surprising kick for a pink drink.

'Mainly sloe gin and vodka,' Angel said, seeing my face. 'I'll get you a proper drink in a minute. Philip has built a bar. Seriously though, he thought he'd got on the wrong side of the village and he knows suspicion is a bad thing to live with. He wanted to show them there's nothing to worry about. We're just all one big, happy family. Personally I think a spot of suspicion keeps life interesting.'

I doubted Philip was making quite the impression he wanted among the Women's Institute and Parochial Church Council members but you had to give him credit for trying. And trying he was, running his makeshift bar from the corner of the courtyard. He had a couple of trestles resting on big oak barrels and was merrily ladling out punch or wine and sometimes a mixture of both, to all comers. Requests for 'a nice cup of tea' or 'something soft please' were met with pained looks but otherwise he was smiling and affable.

We caught up with Ash at the bar. He was downing a glass of wine –'Home-made but not so bad' and lining up glasses for himself and Celia.

'Mrs L won't touch it. Says it's too early for alcohol.'

Reeling from the aftershocks of the punch, I thought she was probably right.

'Make sure you all come and have a look at the workshops before you get pissed,' said Angel. 'I wouldn't want Celia and her mum to miss anything. Come on,

David. We'll see you later Ash.' She took my arm and we plunged back into the crowd.

The workshops were almost as crowded as the courtyard and I wondered if there were bus trips here from Alnwick. There were displays in each of the partitioned stalls, an artist behind each one. They all looked thoroughly pissed off.

'I thought artists liked showing off their work,' I whispered to Angel.

'They do normally. If the audience appreciates them. Philip made them come today, to explain their work. Like anyone cares.' Angel waved at a slim girl, a couple of years older than us, with waist length hair, who was standing to the side of a collection of tiny paintings. 'That's Willow and her wind paintings.'

I'd heard about Willow and her work. I'd amazed my dad, repeating Angel's description of how she would stand in front of her easel for hours 'waiting for the inspiration to blow in. Sometimes she doesn't paint anything for days, even weeks but then, when the creative wind is blowing, she can be in a frenzy and finish three or four paintings in a day.' It took my dad three or four weeks of hard work to complete one of his seascapes. Now I stared at the pretty wind painter and her tiny pieces of art. I bent forward for a closer look but all I could make out on the squares of white cloth, were swirls of blue and green, jewel dots of red and amber and a scattering of silver and gold threads.

'They're very small,' I whispered to Angel. Willow was smiling at me and I found her calm gaze disconcerting.

'These ones are just for selling at things like this. The proper paintings, for the galleries, are much bigger, they can take up a whole wall. The Americans will pay thousands for them, because they know that the wind of inspiration is unpredictable and they don't know when Willow will produce another painting.'

Whenever she needed the readies, I nearly said. Willow was still smiling and I hurried Angel on.

As we pushed our way though the throng some of our neighbours and friends of my parents greeted me. I stopped, to be polite, saying 'hi' and 'yes they'll be along later,' and 'it is terribly hot in here'. I could feel Angel's eyes boring into my back.

'Do you know everybody?'

'No. Just people who live near us or from the pub or who know Mum and Dad,' I replied.

'Well, I'd keep away from me if you want to carry on knowing them. The way they look at me I expect them to cross themselves or throw holy water.'

'Don't talk crap. You're getting paranoid.'

'I am not. And have you seen the way they look at everything? Pretending they're taking it all so seriously and really they're taking the piss.' She turned away, shoulders tense under her thin top. She was right. Behind their polite smiles and tactful comments most of the visitors hadn't a clue what was going on in these workshops. The wild wire sculptures and soup bowls without sides were just too weird. My parents and their friends wouldn't know whether to laugh or be outraged. Some were buying small pieces, in the way they had a go on the tombola at the village fair. They thought they were being kind and I hated them for it.

Angel had had enough browsing.

'Come on. It's time we were getting out of here.' She was peering ahead through the crowds as if she was searching for something. I hadn't finished looking at the exhibits but Angel was moving so quickly all I saw was a blur of primary colours in one corner and a collection of twisted tree roots and moss in another. When I tried to stop, she turned round with an infuriated, 'Come ON!'

Finally we came to a breathless halt. We'd come the length of the stable block and were outside her mother's studio. As were Celia and her mum. They must have been ahead of us all the way but I'd not seen them through the throng.

Mrs Lambert was clutching a weird wooden object and they were clearly trying to find a way out. Angel stepped forward, 'Celia. Celia's Mum. Hi. Have you finished the tour?' There was a thread of ice in her tone that I didn't understand. I saw Celia's eyes widen warily.

'Yes, thank you, Angel. It was actually very interesting. Some most unusual exhibits.' Mrs Lambert looked round her. 'Can we get out this way?'

'What did you think, Celia? You didn't feel contaminated by the Pagan art?' Angel's tone was almost too friendly.

'It was fine. Not my thing. But you know that don't you?'

'Mrs Lambert, you obviously liked Devon's work.' Angel pointed at the wooden object in Mrs Lambert's hands. 'He specialises in fertility symbols. That's a very powerful one you've got. The Horned God as phallic symbol. The phallus as source of all life. You've got good taste.'

Mrs Lambert looked questioningly at her sculpture, 'It does have a certain basic energy doesn't it? What do you think Celia? Will it go well on the mantelpiece?'

Celia ignored Angel's smirk. 'I don't know Mum. Probably not. Let's go and find Ash.' Celia took her mum's arm.

'I expect you'll find him by the bar, he's probably pissed,' said Angel companionably. 'All that phallic power and no way to release it. Are you sure you don't want one of Devon's sculptures for yourself Celia? Might be educational?'

'Angel, shut the fuck up,' Celia's voice shook. Her mum looked confused and started to edge away down the corridor.

'Come on, Celia. We should go.'

'Yes I'd get a move on. You don't want to hang round here. David and I are desperate for a shag.'

I froze. We all froze, except Angel, who calmly unlocked the studio door.

I saw the disgust on Mrs Lambert's face. I couldn't meet Celia's eye but I knew she was waiting for me. To stop it all there.

I didn't. I let Angel pull me into the studio, heard her lock the door behind us. I didn't say a word as Angel removed her blouse and started to kiss me, long and deep. I did nothing, said nothing and God, I had the best sex of my life.

Chapter Sixteen

I left Angel as the sun was setting and she watched me go without a word. I was sodden with sex and shame. The workshops were deserted and in the courtyard only a few plastic cups and the makeshift bar witnessed that the open day had ever happened. I made my way down the drive without seeing a soul. I had lead in my stomach and a drum inside my head, with an overwhelming desire to be clean.

I couldn't go home. Mum and Dad would be there, fresh from the open day, with a raft of questions. Instead I did what Ash would have done and headed for The Plough.

As I waited for Derek to pour my pint he nodded over to the corner of the room, 'Meeting your mate are you? He'll be about ready for another pint. Shall I get you one in for him?' I looked. In the darkest corner of the bar, slumped over his glass, was Ash. He looked worse than I felt.

Resigned, I paid for two pints and took them over. I sloshed one down in front of him and he looked up.

'Oh, it's you.'

'I'll take it back then, shall I?' I reached for his glass but his fingers closed round it.

'You can leave that.' And when I made to sit down, 'I don't feel like talking.'

'Believe me, neither do I.'

So, we sat there, wordless, and after a bit he got up and bought another round.

'What the fuck did you do to Celia this afternoon?' His eyes were bloodshot but he wasn't drunk. Not properly drunk. I swallowed.

'I didn't do anything to her.'

'Ok. What the fuck did you SAY to Celia this afternoon?'

'I didn't say anything. It was...'

'It was Angel. Yeah, I know. But you were there. Well I hope she's worth it 'cos Celia has completely lost it.'

'What d'you mean – lost it?' I picked up a beer mat and started shredding it into tiny pieces.

'I mean you and Angel pissed her off so much that she had a right go at me, in front of everyone, including your mum and dad. And so we've split up. Cheers mate.' He banged his glass down on the table and I noticed his hand was shaking, ever so slightly.

'Don't be stupid. You can't split up over something Angel said.'

'Sod Angel. It's Celia I've had it with. She just doesn't know when to leave something alone. She goes on and on like she has all the answers, like she's the only one who knows what's right and wrong. Well I can't take her frigid morals anymore.'

'Don't talk about Celia like that,' I said quietly.

'Oh, you'll defend her now will you? Shame you didn't feel like that earlier. 'Cos believe me if you think Celia's mad at me that is nothing to how she feels about you.' He gave a short laugh.

'Me?' I tore the mat in half.

'Yeah Mr-Not-So-Innocent all of a sudden. You're Celia's number one target.'

I felt a cold spike of fear, Celia was never angry with me. 'What did she say?'

He took a long swig at his pint, wiped his mouth with the back of his hand and shifted in his seat. Then he directed his comments to the empty fireplace across the room. 'She said how much you'd changed, since Angel turned up and how she felt sometimes you're like a stranger.'

I swallowed, I didn't want to hear this.

'She's right. You have changed. But other than that she's lost the plot. She's freaking out because you and Angel are sleeping together. Like it's any of her business. Just because she's a virgin and keeps me panting round her like a lap dog it doesn't give her the right to slag off everybody else.'

I stared at him.

'Anyway, what exactly did Angel say to her? It had better be good,' he said.

I stared at my pint, ran my finger across a crack in the table. He was waiting. I took a deep breath, 'She told Celia and her mum to go away because me and her were, were… desperate for a shag.' I looked up when Ash started to laugh.

'Angel said that? To Celia? And her mum?' He threw his head back and laughed out loud, his hair falling across his face. To my amazement I found that I was laughing too.

'Yeah, she really did.'

'You fancy a walk?' he asked a bit later and we went out into the soft caress of the warm evening, heading nowhere or anywhere. As we walked Ash told me about what I'd missed at the open day.

'You might have been having the most fun, screwing Angel but I was getting on alright with her stepdad. He's a seriously weird guy but he makes decent wine. Celia and her mum went off to look at the arty stuff and I hung around with Philip. It was actually very pleasant there in the sunshine.' Ash stretched his arms above his head. 'Your dad came over and had a word. Then old Philip decided he'd give a speech, so he got up on the edge of the stone water trough and waved his glass around a bit. He said he hoped everybody had enjoyed themselves and that we all understood each other a bit more. Then he fell off and told me he wished they'd all bugger off home. Your dad thought it was dead funny.'

He would have done and I smiled. Ash continued, 'So, despite being there under protest, I was making the best of it, when Celia and her mum came flying out of the stables like they'd disturbed a nest of killer bees and suddenly everything was my fault.' He kicked a stone viciously into the hedge. 'Mrs Lambert was all fluttery and going on about "that strange girl" and "so embarrassed" and Celia was screaming that she'd told me this would happen and Angel's a slut ...'

'What?!'

'Oh yeah, I know. I stood there and took it but what I really wanted was to slap her. Anyway your dad got hold of her and she calmed down a bit. We stuck her mum on a bus in the village, then, God, we just argued till I told her to stick it. I'd had enough. I'd really, really had enough.' His shoulders slumped and he looked so tired I wanted to put my arm round him, tell him it would be alright.

We walked on in silence and I realised we were approaching the cricket ground, at the edge of the village. Ash pushed open the little lychgate and we sat on the pavilion balcony, feet up on the railing and he lit a cigarette.

'Touch of déjà vu,' he said. 'I was sitting here this afternoon when I told Celia to piss off.'

'Yeah, but why? I know she embarrassed you but none of this is her fault.'

'All of this is her fault.' Ash blew a stream of smoke, which climbed into the roof of the pavilion, blue tendrils unfurling like a creeping plant. 'If she wasn't so fucking frigid, Angel wouldn't get to her so much.'

'Ash! Don't. You don't mean it.'

'No? Maybe I do, maybe I don't, but if she loved me she'd sleep with me wouldn't she? I mean Angel sleeps with you and she doesn't even love you.'

'What the fuck do you know? Leave us out of it.' I stood up, ready to go.

'Well if you believe Celia, Angel's only sleeping with you to get to me. How sick is that?' He started to laugh.

'Ash, shut up. I mean it. I know you're pissed but I don't have to listen to this.'

'It's not me. It's Celia. Your beloved, virginal Celia. She thinks Angel's shagging you to get at me and to stop her being a Christian!'

'She's wrong,' I whispered and sat down again.

'Course she's wrong. God not even Angel's that twisted. It's Celia with the problem. I told her. I said she ought to keep her mouth shut. She's only jealous 'cos you're not pining after her anymore and she's lucky she's kept me hanging on so long.' I thought I caught the slightest tremor in his voice. He ground his cigarette out with the ball of his foot and lit another. He never chain smoked.

'What did she say?'

'Nothing. She just looked at me. Like I'd knifed her in the guts or something. Then she ran off. I wanted to go after her. Say I was sorry.' His voice definitely shook and he turned away from me. 'And I am sorry. I'm really, really sorry.'

Ash was crying. I froze. Then I did what I'd wanted to do since we sat down, I slipped my arm around his shoulders. I expected him to stiffen, shake me off but he didn't. He just sat there, his shoulders shaking and I held him as the darkness deepened over the cricket field.

Chapter Seventeen

I'm surprisingly good at self deception. I didn't see Ash or Celia again for a week after the open day and I convinced myself it was nothing out of the ordinary.

It was a shame I couldn't induce amnesia in my parents. They wanted to talk about the open day – a lot. Mum wasn't so bad, she'd been inspired and didn't need a response.

'I think your dad should become a wind painter,' she announced. 'They've got the right idea at those workshops. Paint something, anything, then claim it's divinely inspired and make sure it's in short supply. Commercial genius. I was talking to that Willow person and she can make £3,000 for one average size painting. It only takes her a couple of hours to knock one out. Your dad's been wasting his time all these years. Wind painting is the way forward. Or what about moon painting? That'd be different.'

I pointed out that Dad probably didn't see either wind or moon painting as the way forward but she was convinced and it stopped her asking awkward questions.

Yes, Mum was fine. But Dad gave me a few nasty moments. Not that he said anything directly, that wasn't his way. He just kept the tap dripping. Water torture.

'Did Ash get Celia home alright? And her mum?' Concerned.

'Ash likes a drink doesn't he? I never realised.' Thoughtful.

'Celia's a lovely girl. Very sensitive, I'd say.' Reflective.

'Hoped your mother and I would see you at the open day. You must have been busy with Angel.'

Give me Mum's thoughtless blathering every time.

Angel certainly wasn't going to pretend nothing had happened. I thought she'd been infected by Mum because she wouldn't shut up either. She wanted to know everything Mum and Dad had said: what did their friends think; were they laughing; did anybody like the art; had I heard about Philip falling off the bar? I told her what I could but it was her questions about Ash and Celia I couldn't answer.

'Have you heard from either of them since?' she asked. We were drinking lattes in the coffee bar in Alnwick, settled in comfy leather chairs in a shadowy alcove, a glass topped table between us.

'I haven't seen Celia at all,' I said. 'Dad said she was upset but obviously he doesn't know why.'

'I bet it was awkward. Didn't your dad want to know what was going on?'

Oh yes. He certainly did. 'No, not really.'

'Oh. But didn't he say anything else? Like if Celia was upset? Or was she just mad? And did he notice how Ash reacted?' She had her elbows on the table, her face framed by her hands.

'He just said that Celia was upset and Ash took her and her mum home. And I haven't seen her since.' I tore the top off a packet of brown sugar and scattered the crystals on the top of my coffee. 'You ought to apologise you know.'

'Whatever. So should you. You've seen Ash though haven't you?'

I watched the sugar crystals melting and subsiding into the latte froth before I stirred them carefully. Angel gave my mug a shove and the foam slopped over the side, 'Tell me what he said then. Did he have a row with Celia?'

'Why would he have a row with Celia?'

'I dunno. So, go on, tell me what Ash said.'

I didn't want to. I really didn't want to tell her anything Ash had confided to me. But I would tell her. Eventually.

'I'll get it out of you,' she said and drained her coffee cup. 'Are we staying here? If so I want another coffee.'

'I'll tell you what Ash said if you tell me the rest of the story about your mum and Philip,' I said, buying time.

'But it's so boring. Go on then, I'll tell you, if you really want.' She waved the waitress over and ordered two more lattes and a chocolate croissant. Then she settled back in her chair, so that the leather creaked and stretched her legs out in front of her, 'Ok, so you've got Sylvia and me on the festival circuit, you've got Philip making his posh pots down the council college in London. How did they come to meet?' She might pretend reluctance but she was enjoying this. 'Philip was, is, actually pretty good at pottery. He started selling a few bits and when the council had a stall at a local craft market he was invited to go and sell his stuff. You can picture the scene can't you? Earnest

101

young potter manning his stall in some godforsaken municipal building, when his whole life is illuminated by the vision of loveliness walking in through the municipal door, complete with snotty faced kid at her side. But I don't think he noticed me. Sylvia says he practically fell at her feet and he hasn't got up properly since. Philip doesn't tell it much differently.

'I don't know the details but he left Pimlico for paradise on the open road and they've never looked back. I'm the last one to believe in happy endings but they are ridiculously fond of each other.' Angel shook her head in disgust.

I laughed, 'You mean they're in love. Still. After all this time?'

'Love. Right. It's just a word. Come on, I'm swimming in coffee and I want to go to the bookshop. While we walk you can tell me what Ash said about Celia. I'll keep the next instalment till I want something else from you.' She smiled but it wasn't a nice smile. I followed her out of the café and as we turned towards the bookshop I reluctantly repeated everything Ash had told me.

She denied everything, of course. And, of course, I believed her. I knew she wasn't sleeping with me to piss off Celia, or Ash. As she said, why would she do that? As for insulting Celia and her mum, 'Yeah, it was crude. But that's just me. I say what I want. But I'm sorry if I've upset them and I'll say I'm sorry if you think it will help. Next time we see Celia.'

Which was all well and good but we didn't see Celia. Sunday came around. We often met up on a Sunday. I would meet Angel first and we'd cut across the fields to the barn and catch up with the others later. I went to meet Angel as usual, thinking that if I kept to our routine maybe the others would too.

I was irritated to see Ash leaning on the church gate as I approached. Angel was sitting on the gate post and they were both laughing, all laid back and relaxed. No tensions between those two then. I was nervous and annoyed at the same time. I hadn't seen Ash since I'd helped him home from the cricket pavilion and passed him into the tight lipped care of his stepmother. Would he remember? They both looked up and smiled.

'Dave, mate, how are you doing?' He didn't remember. 'I came to see if you two wanted to come and have lunch in Seahouses – on me. Dad wants me to take a fishing trip out later and I said I would if he stood us all lunch.' He smiled expansively, enjoying his generosity.

'I said we'd love to go,' said Angel, taking my arm and squeezing it. 'We would, wouldn't we?'

I hesitated. Did this mean no visit to the barn today?

'You don't have to.' Ash's smile faded. 'I just thought it'd be nice. You know after everything that's happened.' He got that pensive look I couldn't resist.

'Yeah, alright. Never turn down a free lunch. When shall we meet you?'

'You have met me. I'm here. We can drive over, have a walk on the front to build up an appetite and then a couple of beers before lunch.'

'You're taking a trip out. You can't drink.' I told him flatly. He shrugged.

'Anyway,' I said, 'we'll have to wait for Celia and if she's gone to church she won't be out for another hour.'

They both stared at me incredulously.

'What? We always wait for Celia,' I said

'Yes, but she hasn't always just split up with Ash,' Angel pointed out.

'They haven't really split up though, have they? It was just a stupid argument over what you did at the open day,' I said.

'What I did? What we did actually.'

She had a point. I still hadn't spoken to Celia. I'd kind of assumed I'd see her today and things would just slip back into place. But nothing was in its place this summer.

In the end we had fun in Seahouses. Lunch was good and Ash and Angel were making an effort to get on. When Ash was making an effort he was the best company in the world. I asked him when he was going to call Celia and he didn't take offence.

'I can't call her. Not after the way she screamed at me. I'll say I'm sorry for what I said but only if she's going to apologise as well.'

'I want to apologise too,' said Angel. 'I just don't think I'll get near enough to have the chance. Her and her mum will be on full Angel alert now.'

'You'll have to call her, Dave,' said Ash. 'She'll always talk to you.'

But I didn't know what to say.

I knew I ought to ring Celia. And I would, when I was ready.

Ash was like a spare part. I knew it was only a temporary rift between them but I never thought he'd miss Celia so much. I couldn't get rid of him. I was used to seeing him most days, when he wasn't working. Now he never seemed to be working and he always seemed to be with me. Which was fine. He was good company. He was my best mate. But I never got a minute alone with Angel. After about five days of wall to wall Ash I complained to her. She just shrugged and said we should carry on as normal and if Ash wanted to tag along then fine.

'We can hardly have him tagging along to the barn can we?' I said.

'Don't see why not?' I never knew when she was joking.

I gave it a week and arranged a night in with Angel. Mum and Dad were going out on a rare evening together and promised not to be back till late. I got Dad's whisky out and committed my allowance to replacing it; fiddled about with the switches to create a bit of mood lighting and put on the music Angel hated least. She arrived promptly wearing a slinky dress and carrying a bottle of wine.

We were locked in a very promising clinch when there was a knock on the door. I ignored it. Another knock and Ash walked in.

'What the fuck!' I sat up abruptly.

Angel half fell off me, giggled and said, 'Hi Ash.' Like nothing had happened. That was the end of my evening. Ash sat down in Dad's chair, poured himself a whisky and put his feet on the coffee table.

'Any crisps going?' he said.

I looked to Angel for help but she just shrugged and turned the lights up.

'Fuck you,' I muttered as I threw a packet of cheese crisps at Ash's head. I had to see Celia, and soon.

Chapter Eighteen

'Okay. I'm sorry. I should have come round earlier. If you want to hurt me make it quick.'

I stood at Celia's front door, with my hands across my head to ward off imaginary blows. Through my arms I could see she was smiling, just the tiniest, edgiest bit.

'Seriously, though,' I let my hands drop to my side, 'I am sorry. I knew you were upset and I should have called.'

'Yeah you should. And you should have told that bitch where to get off when she insulted me and my mum.' No smile now, arms folded, as she leant on the door post.

'Probably. It was just you know…'

'Difficult,' she finished. 'Easier to screw your girlfriend than stick up for your best friend. It's alright David, I get it. Angel comes first.'

I shifted on the step. I'd said my bit and by now I should have been forgiven and invited in. 'Well, I came to say I was sorry and I've said it, so bye.' I started to edge away. I was almost to the gate when she said, 'Did you want a coffee?'

I turned back. Celia was holding the door open, so I shrugged and went in.

She'd only invited me in to talk about Ash. I sat at the narrow, pine breakfast bar and read the reminders on the notice board, 'Buy bread'; 'order eggs for Friday'; 'Dentist!' Celia made coffee in china mugs and tossed me a packet of chocolate biscuits.

'Why didn't Ash come himself?'

'What d'you mean? I came 'cos I wanted to say sorry.'

'Ash didn't send you then?'

'No. But he does want to apologise. He's just been a bit – busy.'

'Yeah. Busy. First time in five years he's been too busy to ring me. Too proud more like. Did he tell you what I said?'

'Yeah. About Angel and stuff?' I didn't really want to get into this.

'He upset me you know? Some of the things he said. About sex – and me.' God, I really didn't want to get into this.

'But he's sorry. He told me he's really sorry,' I said.

'So why isn't he here telling me that? Or does he really want to finish?' She put a cup in front of me and sat down on the next stool.

'No, of course he doesn't! He's in a right mess without you. It's just, well he was upset as well. He said you were pretty horrible and he thinks…' I wavered.

'He thinks I should apologise too. Typical Ash. Never completely in the wrong.' She wrapped her hands round her mug, and hugged it to her. We sipped our coffee in silence.

'Ok. So I'll apologise. He'll apologise. You've apologised. Then what?' Celia said.

'Then nothing. Things go back to how they were. We get on with summer and try and find Ash a place for the autumn. We can't go to uni without him can we?'

'No, we can't.' She looked thoughtful. 'But what about Angel?'

'Angel? She won't be coming to Uni till next year. But she'll come up and visit.' This was going so well. My mind raced ahead with possibilities for our first term in the city.

'She won't bloody visit me!' Celia banged her cup down on the worktop and a stream of coffee arced out and slopped onto the floor. 'Bugger.' She got up to get a cloth. 'I don't want Angel anywhere near me.'

'Ash told you what she's been doing didn't he?' she said as she mopped up.

'Not specifically, no.'

'That she's been winding me up for ages, for not sleeping with Ash, telling me I'm not a proper girlfriend. And slagging Christianity for stopping 'natural' relationships.'

'Oh, yeah. That crap.' She looked startled at my tone. 'And he told me that you reckon Angel's only sleeping with me, to make you look inadequate. You really must think you're important for her to go to all that trouble.' I pushed my cup away and stood up.

'I did say that. But I was upset. You know what she did at the open day.'

'Yeah, and she's sorry. She never meant anything by it.' I crossed the kitchen and looked out at the neat garden and vivid summer borders. 'She's outspoken like that. You know she is. She thinks everyone's as thick skinned as she is. She wants to apologise.' I turned back to Celia.

'Oh, I bet she does. Another convenient apology. And what about all the other stuff she'd been saying to me for weeks now? She's got me so I don't know what to believe any more. I haven't been going to church you know.'

'Yeah, I did know,' I murmured.

'And when Ash said that I couldn't expect him to keep hanging round indefinitely...' She turned her head away and brushed her cheek crossly with one hand. 'But I'm not going to sleep with him. Not to please Ash and certainly not to please Angel. I don't care what you do with her. But I've got my beliefs and they matter. More than your stupid little girlfriend will ever understand.' She squared her shoulders and shook her hair back.

'Ash knows that. He loves you. You know he does.'

'And I love him. But I love God as well.'

'Yeah, alright.' I shuffled my feet on the rustic tiles. 'I'll have to go now. I'm meeting Angel.'

'You're really not going to give her up are you?' Celia stood up.

'No. I love her. And I believe in her. Like you and God.'

We walked to the door and she held it open.

'So?' I asked.

'So?'

'When are we having this apology fest? We can't let it go much longer.'

'I know. Don't push it though.' She gave me a gentle shove out the door. And I had to be satisfied with that.

Chapter Nineteen

At least the open day had some positive consequences. Lord Hedley was convinced he'd won the village over and took to wandering the streets, greeting everybody he met and exuding general goodwill. In turn, the villagers appeared willing to accept the new community as harmless eccentrics. Tentative tolerance began to spread. A couple of the artists started visiting The Plough and even the ladies of the Coffee Circle said 'hello' when they met Willow and her child in the street. I thought it was great, the beginnings of a sixties style love in between village and Hall. Angel told me I was talking rubbish and there wasn't a chance of it lasting.

I didn't care, harmony and reconciliation were in the air. Celia had rung Ash. I didn't know the details but I'd hardly seen him for two days. The next hurdle was to reconcile Angel and Celia. I discussed it with Ash and we decided not to rush it, let them both cool off a bit more.

I don't know whose idea the trip to Lindisfarne was. I'd say Angel's but she didn't know Lindisfarne was Celia's special place. So it must have been mine. Angel thought it was perfect. She'd gone on and on about making up with Celia. I couldn't see why she was so bothered. They'd been good friends early in the summer, but why insult someone you want to be best friends with? I agreed with her though. I missed having the others around. So somehow or other we planned the trip to Lindisfarne. A journey of reconciliation.

Lindisfarne, or Holy Island, was special to me. To us. I'd been loads of times since meeting Ash and Celia. He went because he liked islands, beaches and a selection of good pubs. She loved it for the Christian associations. The Celtic Saints, Cuthbert and Aiden, had lived and prayed on the island and Celia said she could feel their presence there, 'on the breath of the wind.' I didn't believe in saints but there was something special about the place. When the tide swept in over the causeway and the island was cut off for a few hours, I could play the castaway. Celia was right about the air, it was different, a place set apart. And I loved the island because they did.

Angel surprised me. A place of Christian pilgrimage and the ruins of an abbey should have turned her right off. But she was dead keen to go. 'Islands are cool and it'll be perfect for a Pagan rite.'

'Pagan rite? On Holy Island? I thought you wanted to make up with Celia.'

'I do. I don't expect her to be part of it. Or Ash. Or you if you don't want. You can go off and look at dead saints or whatever you do and I can have my celebration on the beach and we'll all be happy. You don't even have to tell Celia what I'm doing if you don't want to.'

'Is it one of those sabbat things, like Lammas?' I asked.

'No, the next sabbat isn't till the end of September. This is just something I want to do. It would be really good if you'd help me with it. It'd make it work so much better. If you don't mind.'

I promised to think about it.

I left it to Ash to persuade Celia to come. If I knew him, he'd leave her feeling that if she didn't come, she'd not only ruin the rest of our summer but quite possibly the rest of our lives. Angel promised to apologise, 'Properly, no sarcasm, honest.'

We drove across the causeway to Lindisfarne early on September 1st. Summer was edging into autumn but we didn't talk about that. Ash still had nowhere to go in October.

The atmosphere in the Land Rover on the drive down was surprisingly light. We met at the Old Vicarage. Ash was unshaven, yawning and looked as though he had a hangover, but cheerful.

He'd been drinking more than usual and I'd given up trying to match him every night. Celia was watchful and withdrawn at first but Angel went straight over to her, looked her in the eye and said, 'I'm sorry Celia. I was rude to your mum and I was offensive to you. I don't know why I did it, maybe I was showing off in front of David.' Celia raised her eyebrows and I exchanged glances with Ash. 'Or maybe not. Maybe I'm just a bitch. But I'm a sorry bitch. You don't have to forgive me but I'd like to be friends. For David's sake.'

Celia shrugged and I held my breath. 'Ok then. I'll let it go. For David's sake.'

Angel nodded and Ash grinned.

She was as good as her word. She did let it go and a casual observer would never have known there was anything wrong between her and Angel. I knew though there was a thread of wariness there, mistrust catching the corners of conversation. I guess Angel knew it too.

We arrived and Ash stopped the Land Rover in a cloud of dust and grit, causing the other visitors in the car park to tut and glare.

'Make sure they know we've arrived,' he said, swinging down from the driver's seat. 'God it's hot again.' It was always hot this summer, I took straight blue skies and relentless sunshine for granted now.

There were a dozen or so cars in the car park already. The tide would flood the causeway in little under an hour so there wouldn't be too many more across. I enjoyed the sense that soon the rest of the world would be stranded on the mainland, relished being trapped on the island.

'Ok, so what's the plan?' Ash asked. 'I don't care what we do so long as I get a crab sandwich at lunchtime with my pint.'

'Make sure it is pint, singular,' said Celia. 'You're driving us home.'

'Dave can drive if necessary,' said Ash.

'No I can't, I've only got a provisional.'

'Yeah, but you can drive. The licence is just a technicality.'

'This discussion is just a technicality,' said Celia. 'You can have one pint and drive us home.'

'You are so good Celia,' said Angel.

'I am aren't I? Why don't we have a walk along the shore to Cuthbert's Isle, bit of time there, back to the village, crab sandwich, pint,' with a pointed look at Ash, 'Abbey, shops, coffee and home.'

'You've got it well organised,' said Angel, not unpleasantly.

'Yeah, it's what we always do.'

'Ok. That's fine with me. I don't want to rock the boat. But what's Cuthbert's Isle?'

I looked at Celia to see if she wanted to explain but she just shrugged and left it to me, 'It's a little islet, a couple of hundred metres off shore. With the tides you can only get across to it a couple of times a day. Saint Cuthbert used to retreat there to get away from the monastery and all the visitors.'

'He prayed there and the birds tended to him. It's a holy place,' said Celia with the thread of a challenge.

'Ok. I get it. But what's actually there?' Angel persisted.

'Nothing,' said Ash. It's a little rocky island with a bit of grass, a few flowers and a cross. I know it well.'

'It's an atmosphere thing really,' I said.

'Well, I want to go to Cuthbert's Isle. It's mainly what I came for.' Celia's jaw was set.

'And I really don't,' said Angel. 'I'm not being awkward or anything but I'm not going to get the Christian vibes am I? And I might spoil it for Celia.' Celia looked as if that was only too likely. 'Anyway,' Angel went on, 'I want to do my own spiritual thing while we're here.'

'A Pagan thing?' asked Ash. 'Like that Lammas stuff you made us do?'

'Sort of. But I'm not going to make anybody do anything. Except David. He said he'll help me. So you two,' and she nodded at Ash and Celia, 'can go and look at your rock and me and David'll do our celebration and we can meet up after. Sorted?'

Celia looked as if she wanted to argue but there wasn't really anything wrong with Angel's plan.

'I thought you'd want to see Cuthbert's Isle again David. You always say how peaceful it is,' Celia tried.

'Cee, he's seen it a dozen times. It won't have changed. Let David go off with Angel and dance round a bonfire if that's what he wants.' Ash put his arm round a resisting Celia. 'You can have me to yourself and tell me about Cuthbert and his birds again.' He grinned at her and she gave him a faint smile. 'And when we've finished all this spiritual stuff I want my pint and my crab sandwich.'

'And I want to buy some mead for my dad,' I put in.

'I've heard there's some good Celtic shops,' Angel said.

'And I'm going to the old Abbey, if anyone wants to join me,' said Celia.

Everyone was smiling at each other and I felt as though a mist had been blown aside.

'Before all that – coffee from the kiosk.' Ash pulled a handful of change out of his pocket.

We sipped our coffees on a bench overlooking the narrow shingle beach, where three or four fishermen were repairing nets outside their black tarred huts.

'I could be a fisherman,' said Ash. 'Out on my boat all morning, mending nets in the afternoon, a couple of pints in the evening. I could settle for that.'

'It'd suit you down to the ground mate,' I said. 'Up before dawn, out in all weathers, sharing your boat with some grumpy, smelly blokes. Oh, yeah it's the life for you.'

'You'd hate it Ash. You'd hate anything where you don't have to use your brain. That's why you need to resit. So you don't have to do a dead end job,' Celia said.

'I don't think being a fisherman's a dead end job.' Angel was swinging her legs on the bench. 'There'd be nothing better than a job which put you in touch with the elements. No crappy working in an office, where you can't breathe. I think you should be a fisherman if you want Ash.'

'Maybe. But I am not – NOT,' and he looked straight at Celia, 'going back to school to resit. I don't need a bit of paper to tell me what I can do with the rest of my life.' He crumpled his cardboard cup in his fist and hurled it at a nearby bin.

Celia wanted to get over to Cuthbert's Isle before the tide came in. I figured she had about three quarters of an hour. Angel said we'd walk along with them and find a suitable place for her ceremony. Celia shot her a sharp glance but kept quiet. Angel was walking next to her and I could hear her asking questions about Holy Island's history, the monastery and the fairytale castle perched on its rocks at one end.

When the path forked Ash took Celia's hand and they set off down the slope towards Cuthbert's Isle.

'See you later,' Celia called over her shoulder.

'Ok, so where is Cuthbert's Isle?' Angel asked, peering after them. I pointed out the rocky islet, stranded among rocks and seaweed just off shore.

'Fine. And where's the nearest bit of beach? For our celebration.'

The nearest strip of sand was a couple of minutes away, just out of sight of Cuthbert's Isle. It seemed private enough for whatever Angel had planned but she looked round and said we'd try further along. Which we did, traipsing from one narrow strip of sand, across springy dune grass to another, very similar strip of sand. I could see Ash and Celia, almost out to the islet, Celia holding his arm as they negotiated the slippy rocks. I smiled. It was nice to see them together. Angel saw me looking.

'About here will do,' she said.

'It's a bit exposed isn't it. I thought these Pagan rites were supposed to be private.'

'Here is perfect.' She dropped her bag on the sand and pulled me down next to her. I expected her to get out her supply of candles and incense and prepared myself for a bit of chanting and praise for the goddess. Instead, Angel started to kiss me. In between kisses she said, 'It's the death of summer.' Kissing.

'The sun is about to start his decline and the goddess will mourn him.' More kissing.

'We are going to celebrate the last throes of their summer passion.' And all the time kissing me deeply, her hand round the back of my head, holding me to her.

'Ok. And how exactly do we do that?' I gasped, pulling away for a second, but I already knew. Angel looked into my eyes, for once totally serious and I felt myself falling.

'We enact their love,' she said.

'Oh hell.' Did I say it or only think it? I knew what she was doing. Behind her I could see Ash and Celia had reached the islet. Ash was at one end, looking out to sea and Celia was in front of the rough wooden cross, her hands cupped in front of her.

'Angel, we can't. I can't.'

'Oh, David you can. You can and you will.' She kissed me again, her lips gentle as spring rain. Desire soaked my spine. Her fingers caressed my face, my neck, my chest under my T-shirt and I was too hard to stop her. Behind her Ash had turned, he was looking straight at us.

I fell back on the powdery hot sand, hate and desire fighting, desire winning all the way. I felt Angel's lips on my chest, her fingers at my belt and I stopped fighting. My eyes were open all the time and the sky was bluer than blue, then shot with sunlight.

Chapter Twenty

Raised voices cut through the blue silence. I sat up, dazed; my hair was full of sand and half my clothes were tangled in a gorse bush. Angel was sitting a little way up the beach, fully dressed and combing her hair with her fingers. The voices clashed in my head again and I looked round, confused. Angel caught my eye and wordlessly pointed across the bay to Cuthbert's Isle.

Oh God. On the rocky islet, in front of the cross, Ash and Celia were screaming at each other. Their arms gestured violently against the horizon, her hair blew black in his face. The light breeze carried their words out to sea but I didn't need to hear, to know what they were saying.

'You did it this time David.' Angel put my thoughts into words. I swung round on her.

'Me? I've done it? You're the one who fucking seduced me.'

She started to laugh and I wanted to cry. I pulled my clothes on, ignoring the burrs and sand chafing my skin and then sat on the sand, my head on my knees. Angel was right. I'd done it this time. She came over and put her head on my shoulder. I wanted to push her away. Part of me hated her. But part of me hated me too and I couldn't push myself away.

'Why Angel? You knew what it'd do to them.' I wasn't angry any more.

'I've done them both a favour. Burst their little bubble, let them into the real world.'

'But I don't think they want to be in the real world. I don't.'

The shouting stopped and I looked up. Ash was making his way back across the rocks and even from this distance I could see his shoulders were set with anger. Celia was sitting with her back against the cross and maybe I could hear her sobbing. The sun was beating my shame into me, branding me a coward. It's hard to be 18 and to despise yourself. To think that maybe you've always been despicable. I'd have sat there all day, sunk in pointless introspection if Angel hadn't nudged me with her elbow.

'Are you going to go and get her or shall I?'

'What?' I had no idea what she was talking about.

'Celia. Ash has left her on that rock and the tide's coming in. I know she won't drown but all the same…'

'Like you care.' I stood up. She was right. The tide had turned and the water was already probing its way across the rocks. Ash had reached the shore and without a backwards glance was striding away. One guess where he was going.

'You'd better go, if you're going or you'll both get stuck.' Angel didn't sound concerned, but she did give me a little push. 'You rescue our damsel in distress and I'll go and find her errant lover.'

'He'll go to the pub. Leave him alone, he'll be fine!' I shouted after her. 'I'd rather you waited for me here.

Shit, Celia.' The tide was streaming in now, the rocks already becoming treacherous in the swarming waters and seaweed which coiled and furled its slippery fronds. I tried to hurry but the sun lashed my back and my ankle wrenched between two stones. The pain recoiled up my leg and I squeezed my eyes shut to blink back hot tears. Out on the islet Celia was still sitting at the foot of the cross, staring blankly out to sea. I shouted at her to get up and come to meet me. She turned her head, fixed me with a venomous look, then turned back to the sea again. Ankle deep in sand and seawater, I swore.

'You can play the bloody martyr if you want but I'm not getting stuck here with you!' I yelled. A few more uncertain steps and my foot touched dry land. I tried to pull Celia to her feet but she resisted, kicking out at me.

'Leave me alone! You've ruined my life. We were so happy and you've let her wreck it all. So just fuck off and leave me alone.'

Anger gave me strength and I yanked her to her feet. 'Now, either you can walk or I can carry you. The choice is yours.'

'Very masterful. Do you practice that with Angel?' Her face twisted in a spasm of dislike. I'd never realised Celia could look ugly.

She came with me. The sea was boiling round our feet and the rocks shifted under us. Celia was forced to hold onto my arm as we staggered across but I could feel her recoiling. It hurt.

When we reached the shore I sat down. Celia stood and looked at me for a minute, 'Who are you?' She shook her head and set off along the path to the village. I let her go and rested my head on my knees. I wanted to sit there forever, submerging my thoughts in the distraction of wet feet and sunburn.

Maybe five minutes, maybe half an hour passed. I heard footsteps on the path beside me and curious voices but they were the voices of strangers and I let them pass without lifting my head. After a while the discomfort stopped being a distraction and I took my shoes off to let my feet dry in the sand. Then the sun got too hot and I started to feel hungry. I wasn't made for self denial and I set off for the village.

The village square was hot and bright, the whitewashed buildings splashed with baskets of flowers. A panting dog drank from a bowl outside the café and tourists in T-shirts drifted between the shops, adding to their collections of Celtic-crossed carrier bags. Off to my right, the ruins of the priory lingered beside the museum and on a bench outside, was Celia. With a sigh I went to join her. She was watching a group of teenagers and I followed her gaze. There were three of them, 15 or 16 years old, with rucksacks and socks rolled down above their hiking boots. They were resting in a pool of shade, two boys and a girl, passing a can of coke between them. The girl wiped sweat from her forehead, as one of the boys fixed her rucksack for her. The other boy leant against the wall and stared across the square, a familiar faraway look in his eyes.

'Oh God,' I said under my breath.

'I guess you're the dreamy one. Or then again you'd probably be helping me wouldn't you, and Ash would be sitting back and watching.' Celia smiled a bitter little smile. 'Funny what a difference one summer can make.'

The trio in the shade tossed their can in the bin and moved off towards the harbour. They passed within a few feet of us and I had an urge to call out a warning. But what could I say?

'We'll have to find the others. I want to go home,' I said.

'I'm sure you do but unless you're planning on swimming, you're going to have to wait. The tide won't go down for another four hours.' Celia sounded resigned but at least she was talking to me.

'What the hell are we going to do for four hours?' I was horrified at the prospect of being trapped here. And where were Ash and Angel?

'I don't give a damn what you do, so long as you keep out of my way. I'm going into the priory so you can go anywhere else. You might want to look for Ash and Angel.' She gave me a strange sidelong look.

'They'll be in a pub.'

'I'm sure they will.' Celia stood up. 'Angel's probably putting stage two into action right now.'

'Stage two?'

'Of her plan. You know, now I'm out of the way.' Her voice wobbled but she shook her hair back and stalked off towards the priory.

I'd have had to find Ash and Angel anyway. I started a search of the darkest corners of the half dozen pubs on the island. I had no doubt Ash would be seeking consolation in the bottom of a glass. It had been the same as long as I'd known him. At first I'd been shocked how much he could down in a session. Later I did my best to match him. The only rule was, never try to stop him. Celia knew the rule. He could usually drink himself into the abyss and out the other side, if he wasn't disturbed. If you tried stopping him he was vicious.

When I found him in the third pub he was deep in the abyss and the other side was several drinks away. He was on the whisky which was a bad sign. Angel must have figured out the rule because there was a trail of empty glasses and he was still letting her sit with him. Sitting very close, with her hand on his shoulder.

I watched them from the doorway but they didn't move, Ash stared into his pint, Angel quiet beside him. For a sliver of a second I felt I was intruding but then I was across the room, making as much noise as possible and watching Angel's hand slip from his shoulder as she turned to greet me. Ash was oblivious.

'There you are,' Angel smiled and reached for my hand. I let her take it and she pulled me down onto a stool next to her. 'I was going to send out a search party. He,' she jerked her thumb towards Ash, 'is in a right state. I don't know how he's staying upright. I think you're going to have to risk that provisional and drive us home.'

I nodded. 'He always drinks when things go wrong.'

'He always drinks. Haven't you noticed?' She leaned forward and brushed her fingertips across my face. 'I'm glad you've come to find me. I thought you were angry.'

'I was. I am.' I breathed in her heavy perfume and wished she would keep on brushing her fingers across my skin like that. I leant forward to kiss her.

'Have you managed to lose Celia then?' Ash said, struggling upright. Angel slipped out of reach.

'I've lost her and a good job too. Maybe now I can have a proper girlfriend and have some proper sex.' He paused, glass raised, struck by his own thought, 'Funny that... proper, Celia was too proper for her own good. Don't know why I stuck with her so fucking long.' He subsided back in his chair and started to laugh.

I was hot, my ankle hurt, I'd been used by my girlfriend to humiliate my best friend and I was stuck on this island for another four hours. I couldn't stop the scalding words which poured out, 'You stuck with her so fucking long, as you put it, because you said you loved her. You claimed she was the only one who could keep you sane and it looks like you were right 'cos you've only been without her for an hour and look at you! You're pathetic Ash, bloody pathetic!' I stood up. 'Come on Angel, let him drink himself to death if he wants.' I took hold of Angel's arm and tried to pull her up.

'Get off!' she pushed me away. 'There's no point taking it out on me. And there's not much point taking it out on him either.'

'Alright but let's get out of here. Go for a walk, have an ice cream, anything till the tide goes out.'

'We can't leave him like this can we?' It was more a statement than a question. 'You have your walk and your ice cream and while you're at it, find Celia. We'll meet you at the Land Rover when the tide goes down.'

It was a reasonable suggestion. I very much wanted to leave Ash to choke on his own vomit but I couldn't do it. He needed babysitting. And someone would have to round up Celia. But I didn't want Angel to stay with Ash.

'Why don't I stay with Ash and you go and get some fresh air and bring Celia along?' I suggested.

She fixed me with a withering look. 'And Celia's going to come skipping along with me, isn't she, 'cos I'm her best friend in the whole world just now. Look, stay here for a bit, have a drink then go and find Celia.' She patted my hand.

'Forget it. I need some fresh air. I just hope he can walk to the car.' I shook her hand away and walked out, pretending I didn't hear her say 'Don't I get a kiss then?' I'd had enough kissing.

It was a miserable afternoon. I ate a bag of crisps and queued for a synthetic ice cream. I walked to the castle and back; I drummed my heels on an upturned boat and waited for the tide to subside. I felt like King Canute in reverse.

I didn't have to look for Celia. She found me slumped in the village square.

'Are we leaving then?' She loomed over me.

I looked up and shaded my eyes to see her face. It was implacably hostile. I nodded and dragged myself after her.

Ash was propped in the back seat of the Land Rover and Angel was sitting on the bonnet. Celia got in the front without a word and Angel climbed in beside Ash. Reluctantly I took the keys and, praying that we didn't get stopped by the police, drove our happy party home.

Part Three

Mabon

Chapter Twenty-one

The communion wafer cleaved to the roof of my mouth and began to dissolve. When the Vicar passed me the communion cup I had the urge to take a deep swig, to wash away the wafer. But I refrained and took a tiny sip, just like the papery lady kneeling beside me.

'Amen,' she said loudly and stood up. I mumbled something which could have been amen and followed her back down the aisle. As I slipped into my pew the papery lady patted my hand and settled herself behind me. I was a bit shaky. My heart had drummed its own beat all the way to the communion rail and back. Was this the cost of forgiveness?

Celia was kneeling at the altar rail now. I saw Rev Armstrong placing the wafer on her tongue, her dark head bowing devoutly. When she came back her face was composed and peaceful. She passed me without a glance and I tried not to mind. At least she had her faith back. I wished I had a faith left to salvage.

Angel had gone to Edinburgh with Willow. She didn't tell me, her sister Sasha did when I finally rang the Hall. She'd gone to help Willow with an exhibition, Sasha didn't know how long they'd be gone. 'Ages, I hope,' she said.

And Ash was gone too, at least for the weekend. He and Caroline had driven up to Ayr to see his grandparents. I should have remembered, they went every year.

It was a relief to be on my own, to have a break from making excuses for us all. Mum grabbed her opportunity and took me shopping in the city. Realisation had slowly dawned on her that I'd be leaving for Uni in a few weeks and she discovered a million things I didn't have and couldn't possibly leave without. She drew up a list. It went on for three pages and I couldn't tell her I didn't want most of it. I knew there was no chance we'd get past the first two or three items anyway.

I was right. One look at my goth gear and Mum almost didn't leave the house.

'Do you have to wear eyeliner, David? It isn't very masculine.' The fact that Ash wore it didn't cut any ice. She was paying so I took her to my favourite clothes shop first and persuaded her to buy me two pairs of ripped black jeans and a T-shirt with mock bloodstains. She needed a cup of tea to recover from that and we pretty much came to a stop in Debenhams' restaurant. I sat back and half listened to her rattling on about the ridiculous price of things, how busy the shops were, that you couldn't breathe in these big shopping centres and did I think I'd be able to get the rest of my things myself. I reassured her and she suddenly stopped in mid flow and took hold of my hand. Quiet alarm passed through me.

'I will miss you David. I know I seem busy all the time.'

'You are busy all the time.'

'Yes I know. I like to be busy. But I will miss you.'

Oh God she was welling up. I patted her hand and said of course she'd miss me and I'd miss her and Dad and did she want another pot of tea while I went in the record shop next door. It was nice of her to say it though.

As usual Dad didn't say anything but he did ask me to go painting with him. When I was a kid we'd gone all the time. He'd sit with his paintbox and easel and I'd mess about with my kite or build dams in the stream or just lie on my back and dream. When I got older I found excuses not to go but he never stopped the invitations.

We went up to St Abbs, a headland near Berwick, where he was painting a commission. We parked in a lay-by near the top of the cliffs and shared Mum's prawn sandwiches, congratulating ourselves on having persuaded her to make them.

'It's because you're going away,' Dad told me.

While he painted I lay on my front at the edge of the cliff and let my eyes roam down to where the rocks met the sea in a protest of foam and spray. Seagulls swooped and recoiled inches above the water, timing their dives perfectly every time. Was it confidence that made you choose to live within an inch of disaster, or blind stupidity?

I wanted Angel. I'd never gone so many days without seeing her, touching her. When I dropped her at the Hall gates, after the Holy Island fiasco, she'd just smiled and said 'see you around', before disappearing into the dusk. I was left to dump Ash on his doorstep, not hanging round to provide explanations. Celia had already jumped ship at the crossroads, preferring to walk two miles home across the fields than spend another two seconds in our company.

Now Angel had decamped to Edinburgh, without a word. It didn't surprise me, but I missed her. Awake at night, with moonlight drenching my sheets, all I could see and taste and touch was Angel. I masturbated but it left me dry and unfulfilled, my head still clouded with unrepentant angels.

In the shopping centre with my mum, every second girl had reminded me of my girl, a scarf twisted through blond hair, skirts skimming the floor, a certain attitude as she turned. All the world seemed artificial, cellophane wrapped for kiddies, bright and shiny, coloured like candy. And me in the real world, which was monochrome and harsh to the touch, because Angel wasn't there.

I walked to Preston Tower, to get some exercise, to shake my thoughts into order and to think about Angel. Climbing over the gate, in the late afternoon, I remembered the Lammas celebration here, as though it belonged to another country.

The tower was unlocked. It sometimes was in summer, there was nothing to steal. I climbed up inside, my feet dwarfing the narrow steps which spiralled away above me. I felt like I was inside a giant helter-skelter and soon I would reach the top and push off, childlike, speeding round and round, back to earth. Instead I climbed three last wooden steps and emerged from the half light. The tower had been built for security, designed to protect whole families from the marauding Scots, pouring in torrents over the Borderlands. The walls came up to my chest but I climbed up and sat astride the thick grey stone, the countryside opening up like a picture book in front of me. A light breeze tugged at my shirt and hair and I felt the late sun's rays stroking the tension out of my shoulders.

I traced the contours of the land below me. The church was the first landmark and then, a little way to the left, the Old Vicarage, solidly built stone, even from this distance. I wondered when Ash would be back. What I would say to him. Him and Celia were finished. Even I couldn't make a happy ending for them now. I let my thoughts brush over Ash, what he would do without a college place, without Celia, and I looked instead for the Hall. I followed the wandering line of the wall, working out where the old door into the lane would be, making out the main gates. Angel, come home to me, I breathed into the afternoon. I didn't want there to be another day without her. Far too soon I was going to have to go to uni, to leave the village, to leave Angel.

And what about Celia? I knew what Angel had done but I didn't think she'd had a plan, just reckless indifference. She'd destroyed Ash and Celia's relationship and I still loved her. The sleepless nights since Lindisfarne told me that. Now I knew why the wives of murderers stood by their men; why husbands took back cheating wives just one more time. Love is an unrelenting master, it will not let you go and while it makes you forgive, it refuses to forget.

I tried, but I couldn't see Celia's house from here, it was too far away, hidden in the blue mist of distance. 'I'm sorry Celia,' I said. 'I'm so sorry, but I can't let her go.' I'd loved Celia chastely, purely, pointlessly for so long. It felt almost noble to sacrifice her now for my crimson, carnal love. Pale, perfect Celia. And Ash too. If I sacrificed Celia now, there would still be Ash. I threw my love for her and all my regrets over the ramparts and maybe the wind came and took them or maybe they fell to the ground and were shattered forever.

I walked home through lengthening shadows, enjoying a Victorian melancholy and when I walked through the door of the cottage Dad told me Celia had called.

Chapter Twenty-two

'She wants you to meet her tomorrow, at 2pm in Alnwick,' Dad told me before I'd closed the door behind me. 'I said you'd be there.'

The enjoyable ache of melancholy dropped away, usurped by annoyance. Who did Celia think she was, summoning me to an appointment? Why couldn't I just call her back later? Or she could come round to see me?

'She's your best friend,' Dad was saying. 'She really needs to speak to you and she thinks it would be better on neutral ground.' He pushed a scrap of paper into my hands, confirming the time and place in his copperplate hand. I gave him a close look but he didn't say anything else. What has she been telling you?

'Fine.' I took the bit of paper and slammed upstairs. I put a CD on, one Dad hated and turned the volume up, so I couldn't hear his pleas to turn it down.

I couldn't complain about Celia's choice of venue. Barter Books was a huge secondhand bookshop, housed in the old Alnwick railway station. Room after room of echoing ceilings and aged wooden floors and on every side bookshelves, overwhelmed with volumes on everything. I loved the books, I loved the railway nostalgia and I loved the squishy leather chairs, the real fires and the homemade buns on sale by the coffee pot. The three of us had spent wet afternoons and frosty mornings sprawled on the cracked sofas with toffee cookies and battered novels.

Celia was waiting for me. She wore a long green skirt and a black T-shirt and looked terribly serious. She poured me coffee from the pot on the hot plate and I took a chocolate muffin, dropping coins into the wall safe. I followed her through three or four book-lined rooms, balancing my cup as I side stepped the browsers. She stopped in what had been the waiting room, in the days when trains pulled into a busy station, and closed the door behind us. No-one ever came into the waiting room, there were no books. No books but a few sepia prints behind cracked glass and the original benches – very hard. We sat side by side, coffee and cakes between us and it felt like we were on some prim Victorian picnic, waiting for a train to carry us off to a genteel seaside resort. Celia didn't look as though she'd want me to share the image.

'I wanted to see you because I'm going away for a bit and I couldn't leave things the way they are,' Celia said.

'Going away? Where? For how long?' And even as I didn't want her to go I was thinking how much easier it would be if I didn't have to juggle my loyalties.

'Just to my auntie's, in Dunbar. She's always asking me and I never wanted to go for more than a day or two.' Never wanted to be away from Ash. 'I'll come back in time to pack for college.'

'Will I see you? Before we go to college?' I couldn't imagine leaving without seeing her. And she was supposed to be there when I arrived, at the art college just across the city from me, from Ash.

'I don't know. I might not want to see you. I'm only seeing you now because I hate leaving things unsaid. It gnaws away at me.' She'd always been the same, having to iron out the wrinkles, never going to sleep on a misunderstanding. Until now. Unless she was a chronic insomniac.

'I hate who you've become.' Harsh words and only the prickle of guilt kept me from walking straight out. 'I'm sorry but I do. You were my best friend – after Ash of course.' Of course. 'And you let Angel mess me up – you helped her. No, don't say anything, just let me finish.' She pressed her palm against my chest and I was silent. 'I know what Angel's done to me and Ash and I know it was deliberate. I'm not going to try and convince you, you believe what you like. But just think of this. When summer started, before you ever met Angel, did you think anything could split me and Ash up? Anything at all? Whether we were sleeping together or not?'

I shook my head. There had never been a picture of the future without those two together, somewhere in the foreground.

'And look at us now. The only change in the mix is Angel, and you falling for her right on cue.'

'And that was wrong? It was OK for you to have Ash but not for me to have someone? Is that what you're saying?'

'No. It's not. You should have someone.'

'But not Angel?'

'Not Angel, no.'

The door clattered open and a middle aged couple with walking boots and earnest expressions came in. Celia turned away, gazed out of the window onto the car park and I was left to go to the door and point them towards the travel section. When I came back Celia took my hands in both of hers. 'I know you love Angel. I know you won't believe the worst of her and you won't give her up. But please listen to me. Angel has her own agenda. I'm only part of it and I'm pretty sure you're only part of it too. So be careful.'

I gave a non-committal shrug.

'I'll keep in touch. I know you didn't really want any of this. But promise me one thing.'

'What?' Wary.

'Look after Ash.'

'I think he's old enough to look after himself.'

'You know that's not true. Promise me you'll look out for him. Because we both love him and that's the one thing that won't change, isn't it?'

She must have got up got up then and left. I have a vague recollection of her bending to kiss my cheek, but maybe that's only what I wanted her to do. I stared at the door after she'd gone. I loved them both. And that wouldn't change.

Chapter Twenty-three

When I got back from Alnwick Ash's bedroom window was ajar. He was home then. I strolled over and Caro answered the door.

'He's in the shower,' she said, so I told her I'd see him for a pint later. As I was leaving, I asked her if Ash had sorted anything for autumn. She pulled a face and shook her head.

'Granddad says he can get him a job with Uncle Graham but you know what Ash is like.'

I did. Uncle Graham was senior partner in a big firm of Edinburgh accountants. Ash would rather die than work for him.

He was a bit morose walking to The Plough but cheered up after a couple of pints. I avoided the C word until he mentioned her and when I said she was going away he just shrugged. He asked where Angel was and I told him she was away with Willow. All the time I watched him, twisting his glass between his hands and shaking his hair out of his eyes, habits as familiar as my own. I couldn't imagine not being near him. I wasn't ready for Angel to come home.

The talk among the regulars was all about the Hall. Derek suspected a couple of the artists had been smoking pot in the back room of the pub.

'I won't have drugs. Lose my licence like that,' and he snapped his fingers high in the air, 'if the police get a whiff of drugs around the place. I didn't catch them at it but there was that smell, you know?' And half a dozen blokes who'd never smelt dope in their lives, nodded sagely. 'If I smell it again, I'll have to ban them.'

'You'll have to ask Angel if she's got any to spare,' Ash grinned.

I left The Plough just after eleven. I'd had enough and I wanted to clear my head. Ash stayed on, hopeful of a lock in. Derek occasionally obliged when the right people were there.

It was a glorious night. The moon was full again, weaving in and out of shreds of cloud above the church tower. The village street was dusty and the air still, anticipating another scorching day. I came level with the Hall gates and kept walking. But then a light caught my attention, flickering across the driveway like a flashlight then disappearing. Despite myself, I slowed down. The drive was sunk in darkness but there was the sense of movement ahead and I thought I heard voices, muffled laughter. Four or five pints encouraging me, I set off to explore.

I hadn't played at being a spy since I was eleven. Now I glided from straggly bush to overgrown shrub, edging up the drive, imagining I was both graceful and noiseless. As I neared the house the pools of shadow shrank and a lake of golden light spread from the front stairs towards where I crouched behind an ancient conifer. The whole community must have been there, a dozen or more people busy round two vans, lifting and carrying boxes. I saw Philip, directing operations from the top of the steps, his grey ponytail come loose so his hair wafted around his face like smoke. Sylvia was beside him, head swathed in a red turban, opening the door whenever someone staggered up the steps, bowed under a load of boxes and metal frames. Three or four kids were messing about by one of the vans. I guessed Angel's siblings were there; maybe the girl with the patchwork skirt was Carmen; the little boy with a bandanna, Kenzie. Questions about what they were unloading were overwhelmed by the big question, where was Angel? And did I really want to see her?

The last of the cargo must have been unloaded because a big bloke with a waistcoat over his bare torso slammed the doors of the first van and strode towards the house. Most of the others followed him, Pied Piper like, and Philip and Sylvia disappeared inside. The kids were left, kicking something round in the dust. I started to back away into the deeper shadows, when a voice snapped, 'Kenzie, get out of there. Bloody brat.'

I knew that tone and slid back to the conifer. The artist woman, Willow, was emerging out of the back of the second van, her arms piled high with big rolls of paper or canvas. Kenzie was trying to pull out the bottom roll and the whole pyramid trembled. Then Angel stepped round the side of the van, grabbed Kenzie by his checked bandanna and flipped him onto the ground. He gave a

143

banshee shriek and Angel kicked him. He rolled over and ran for the house, the other kids in shrieking pursuit.

'I hate those kids,' Angel said as she steadied Willow's load. Willow tottered off and Angel leaned back against the van, alone now. She pushed her hair out of her eyes, then fumbled in her jeans pocket before lighting a cigarette. She took a deep drag and rested her head against the roof of the van. My eyes brushed over her pale cheeks; stroked her neck and shoulders, down past her narrow waist, her hips and thighs. She was so beautiful. I wanted her with a violence that knocked my breath from my chest and I was sure she must hear me gasp. But she carried on smoking, face tilted to the moon. After a bit she dropped her stub and ground it under her heel. She hesitated, eyes suddenly watchful. I was sure she could sense me and I got ready to step forward, into the light. But she shook her head and went inside and I walked home down the middle of the driveway in the dark with no-one to care if I was seen.

That was it then. One glimpse of Angel and no way I was giving her up. I discarded Celia's warnings like paper in the breeze.

Angel hated me to phone her at the Hall. The next day I rang her anyway and to my amazement she answered. Even more surprising she didn't moan that I'd called her and suggested that we meet, at the Churchyard gate. I bounced out of the house and down the quiet lane as if summer had started all over again.

I was there first and took up the vantage point on the gate post. I could see her approaching from quite a way off and I waved. Maybe she didn't see me, she seemed sunk in thought. Certainly her face was serious as I jumped off the post and kissed her.

'Shall we go for a walk?' she said.

'I thought you hated walking?'

She shrugged, 'If you don't want to walk we won't, I just thought it might be nice. As we haven't seen each other for a while.' Still such a serious expression.

'I'm good for walking. Let's walk,' I said.

So we walked. For almost an hour in the fields behind the Hall, beside standing corn which ticked in the heat, overripe for the harvest. She let me hold her hand as we drifted through the dust of a long dry season. We didn't talk much but when I caught her eye she smiled at me.

Maybe it was deliberate but the way I chose took us back past the old barn. Maybe my footsteps slowed, maybe she caught the question in my eye, but as we came level with the weathered doorway she said, 'ok then,' and we went in.

It was just like all the other times, the caresses, the moans, the straw sticking in my back. It was just like all the other times until I opened my eyes, just before I came, and saw her eyes, expressionless, focussed on something a long way from the barn and our bodies moving together. She rocked rhythmically above me and from her throat came the tiny cries which turned me on, but she wasn't there. Even as we came, together, I felt a space open up inside my chest, a space where everything was slightly off centre, knocked out of true.

We lay side by side in the straw and I had nothing to say. All the little endearments, the love talk was dead on my tongue. I couldn't even slide my arm around her and hold her close. I wondered how soon we could leave. Angel reached over me to grab her clothes and I thought she was going to get dressed and go. I desperately wanted her to stay. Instead she reached inside her short's pocket and pulled out two thin, hand-rolled cigarettes and a lighter.

'Here, maybe this'll stop you taking everything so bloody seriously.'

'I don't smoke,' I said automatically as I took the spliff and let her light it from hers.

'Nah, nor do I.' She propped herself on one side and blew out a thin stream of blue smoke.

She'd never offered me pot before. I lay back and inhaled, ignoring the burning in my chest, concentrating on the tightening of my scalp, the slow blurring of my thoughts. The silence lengthened, expanded but now it was a friendly silence, a shared silence. I started to smile.

'I never wanted to go to Wales you know.' Angel blew a thoughtful stream of smoke towards me.

'No?'

'No. I liked moving about and Philip wanted us to settle down. If you can call joining a commune settling down.'

'I thought Sylvia liked life on the road,' I said.

'She did but she'd had Sasha by then and she was expecting Kenzie, and Philip thought children needed stability. He tries but he can't leave his background behind.' She shook her head sadly.

'What was it like, living in a commune? Was it all free love and dope?'

146

'What, a bit like this barn!' she laughed. 'I loved the commune. I hated the idea of it but when we got there I loved it. There were no rules. No families. Everybody lived by their own ideals. I could pretend I didn't have a mother or a step dad or bratty kid sister. I went to school when I wanted and I learned what I thought was useful and people listened when I talked. And then every summer I went away to the festivals, without Sylvia or Philip.' Her voice took on a nostalgic tone and it was hard to believe this was Angel.

'Who did you go with? You can't have been very old.'

'Twelve, my first summer and then every year until – until this year and I'm stuck in this bloody village. I should have gone anyway. I could have met up with everyone on the road. But I promised I'd be good.'

'Promised who?' I wanted to know but Angel rolled over and assembled another spliff.

'Join me?' She sat up and her breasts gleamed white in a slant of sunlight through the broken roof tiles. I joined her and we sat together, bumping hips and shoulders as our coils of smoke merged and spiralled into the rafters. When she asked how Ash was it was the most natural question in the world.

Chapter Twenty-four

And then there were three. It was fine. It was more than fine. For about three weeks we had a really good time. It felt like the tension had been drained away and the three of us were floating in a late summer bubble. The sun still shone but the evenings were lengthening and the unmistakable whiff of autumn gave every day a special poignancy, so that we felt we couldn't waste a single one.

Angel was right to include Ash now that Celia was gone. We had room for three of us, in some ways it was like the old days with me and Ash and Celia. He didn't irritate me so much now, didn't seem to be in the way. In fact he went out of his way to make sure I had time with Angel. He was always saying, 'I'll get off now and leave you two alone. See you in The Plough later.' I'd lost the urgency to be with Angel every second anyway. Our relationship was maturing. I realised it didn't have to be all about sex.

Angel asked me if I minded Ash being about. 'You're not going to get jealous are you?'

I had nothing to be jealous about. I believed in Angel and I trusted Ash.

It was a golden September. Lying on a rug in the sand dunes, beer in one hand, joint in the other, I was always just on the verge of a profound discovery. The meaning of life almost unrolled for me but I could never quite capture that essence of the thought which would make sense of everything. One day I did manage a whole thought, when it occurred to me that we were smoking rather a lot of pot.

'Isn't it costing you a fortune Angel? Shouldn't we contribute or get our own or something.'

'Like you'd know where to get it,' she said. 'There's bags of the stuff at the Hall. Literally – bags of it.' She sent a smoke ring into the sky and I watched it dissolve, like my thoughts.

'Won't anybody mind us having it?' For some reason this was very important.

'Probably won't notice it's gone. And I don't care if they do. What they gonna do? Report me to the police?'

Ash laughed and cracked another bottle of beer. 'D'you want another one Dave?'

I thought about it for a bit then fell asleep. When I woke up I had sand in my clothes and a sunburned nose. Ash and Angel were nowhere in sight. The remains of our picnic were scattered round me, empty beer bottles half buried in the sand, crisp packets and a sandwich wrapper weighted down with stones. I had a headache coming on but had to tidy up. I was stuffing the last packet into a carrier bag when Ash materialised beside me.

'Celia would be proud of you. Tidying up like that.'

'Where's Angel?'

'Dunno. She went off to meditate or something. You were asleep so I went for a walk.'

'A walk?'

'Yeah. A walk. There was nothing else to do. I wasn't sleepy and you wouldn't catch me sitting cross legged and going ommm.'

I grinned, 'I dunno. I see you as the guru type. Grow your hair a bit longer, maybe a goatee and spout some crap. You'd have them paying to see you.'

'Well, I need a new direction don't I?'

Angel came back then, sauntering along the beach in her flimsy summer dress, swinging her sandals in one hand, her face lifted towards the sun.

'There's one who can play the part,' Ash said.

'What do you mean?'

'Hippy sun child. She's got it off to an art.'

'It's not an act. It's what she is,' I said, surprised. 'You know she believes in all that Pagan sun worship.'

'When it suits her. I reckon she'd rather be playing Lady of the Manor if she got the chance.'

I gave him a pitying look. He really had no idea.

Mum reckoned there was something going on at the Hall. She'd seen vans arriving when she got up for a glass of water in the night.

'A convoy. Five or six vans. Big ones and dark colours – navy or black. Less conspicuous.'

Dad wasn't so sure. 'Probably just delivering some art supplies or furniture,' he said. He was at the kitchen table, trimming the edges of a mount.

'Furniture? In the middle of the night? I don't think so. It was definitely something illicit. Don't you agree, David?'

I raised my hands in a show of ignorance and backed out of the kitchen. I didn't mention the vans I'd seen unloaded, the night Angel came home.

Celia rang me one Tuesday evening. I was happy to hear her voice and took the phone into the back garden, where I sat on the wall, watching the swallows swoop and soar round the chimney pots. A faint smell of dinner drifted out of the house and I could hear Mum clattering pans inside. It wasn't a good line and Celia's voice kept receding so I had to strain to hear her. I didn't have to strain too much to realise she'd called to check up on Ash. My pleasure faded.

'He's fine,' I told her. 'Why wouldn't he be?' Well, I felt like being cruel. 'I'm fine too in case you were wondering. And Angel. She's fine. We're all fine together.' The conversation didn't last long after that and I spent the time before dinner kicking bits of cement out of the garden wall.

I kept hearing her voice though, asking what Ash was going to do next. Has he got college sorted out? Is he looking for a job? What did she want me to say? Tell the truth? No to college, no to a job, no to any plans for the future. Ash is fine. We're all fine together.

Chapter Twenty-five

The Plough was our second home. Ok, it wasn't the most exciting venue but when you live in a small village you take what you can get. There wasn't a whole lot of choice for two goths and whatever Angel decided to be.

Landlord Derek had pretty much left us alone to have a quiet drink and keep out of trouble since we were sixteen. Teenagers made up a good quarter of his clientele. In exchange for no ID requests we kept our heads down, didn't get too blindingly drunk and only threw up in the bar once a year or so. We couldn't risk getting thrown out of The Plough. Correction, I couldn't. Angel didn't give a toss.

When she lit the first spliff I glared at her and signalled for her to put it out. It was alright in the barn or on the beach but not where my dad was likely to walk in.

'You can't smoke that in here.'

'Legally I can't smoke it anywhere. Do you have a particular objection to in here? You've never complained before.'

'You've never tried to smoke in public before,' I hissed. Ash was at the bar getting a round in and I arrowed a need for support at his back. He carried on chatting up Bethany, the new barmaid.

'Don't frown like that. He's a single bloke now.' Angel blew a stream of smoke in my face.

'I'm not frowning. He can do what he likes, but Bethany's seeing Simon Craig.' And then there's Celia.

'Bet that doesn't stop him. But I want my drink now. Go and fetch him over.'

'Ok, but put that out will you.'

'Put that out will you,' she mimicked.

I tapped Ash on the shoulder and reached round him to collect my pint. I smiled at the barmaid. She was very pretty. 'Hi Bethany,' I said, 'meeting Simon when you're finished?'

She flushed scarlet. 'Er no, not tonight. He's gone to his brother's in Edinburgh.' And she started rearranging the clean glasses behind the bar.

'I'll see you later then shall I?' Ash called across to her, 'I'll be here till closing.' She blushed again and dipped her head.

'She's got a boyfriend you know,' I said as we carried our drinks back across to Angel.

'Yeah well he's in Edinburgh. And I haven't got a girlfriend so technically I'm not doing anything wrong. And don't shake your head like that. You're not my granddad.'

We settled with our pints and pushed Angel's pint of cider over to her.

'Cheers. Fancy a smoke, Ash?' She reached into her bag. Her joint was burning down on the edge of the ashtray.

'Angel don't be bloody stupid.' I reached across and try to wrest the bag off her. 'You're going to get us arrested. It is illegal you know.'

'It is illegal you know,' she repeated, in a sing song voice. 'Here.' She passed the joint to Ash and he put it between his lips and leaned towards her.

'Light?' he muttered and she leaned over, pressing the tips together. They made me sick.

'Didn't some of your lot from the Hall get thrown out for smoking that?' I said.

'My lot? You mean Jake and Kris? Yeah they did. No loss to them.'

Maybe if I ignored them they'd get bored. Maybe Derek wouldn't notice. Maybe Mike Kent's pigs would rise up from their sty and fly in formation over The Plough.

'Is that what I think it is?' Derek loomed into our corner. I was pleased to see Ash quietly stubbing out his joint under the table. Angel put her head on one side and thought for a bit. 'I don't know. What do you think it is?' she said conversationally.

'I think it's stuff that I don't want to see in my pub. So hand it over and we'll leave it at that. These two are good customers, no need for a fuss.' He held his hand out. Angel looked at him.

'It's ok. I'll hang onto it if you don't mind. I might want another one later.'

I thought Derek's eyebrows were going to disappear into his receding hairline. 'You'll not be having another in here. Hand it over or get out.'

'Oh come on Derek. She's only having a laugh,' Ash said. Then Derek saw the remains of his joint.

'You as well. I thought better of you. And you David, wait till I see your dad,' he shook his head. 'You know I

154

turn a blind eye a lot of the time and I don't care what you get up to away from here but you're taking the piss now. Come on, get out.'

'I'm not smoking. It's nothing to do with me. I told them to stop.' I knew I was bleating and Angel gave me a look.

'Come on Ash, we're going.' She took a long drag on her joint then stubbed it out carefully in front of Derek.

'Yeah, think it's time we left.' Ash got up to follow her. 'Hey Beth, I'll meet you back here closing time,' he called across the bar.

Then over his shoulder to me, 'You coming?'

I looked at Derek, arms folded, face impassive then I got up and followed them out into the warm summer night. Angel was hanging onto Ash's shoulder and laughing till I thought she'd be sick.

'Nothing much to laugh about, Angel,' I said as I started to walk home, not waiting for the words to come echoing down the empty street after me.

It was the third week in September and the weather showed no signs of breaking. Angel decided to forgive me and invited me and Ash to a party at the Hall.

'It's for Mabon, sort of Pagan harvest festival, but we're just having a party, no rituals or anything so you should be safe.'

We were all in the barn. I didn't see why we had to share it with Ash but there weren't many places we could go, so I put up with it. Angel was sitting on the edge of the hayloft hatch, swinging her brown legs in time with some inner music. 'So, you both coming?'

'Nothing else to do on a Thursday night,' Ash said. 'We need to bring any drink or anything?'

'Won't go to waste. But don't bother about food. Sylvia and Willow are sorting all that. I keep out of it, can't do with cooking.'

'Perfect little wife you'll make,' said Ash.

'Yeah, well good job I'm not planning on getting married then isn't it? Got to go. See you both Thursday.' And she swung down onto the ladder and disappeared.

'Angel, won't I see you before then?' I shouted after her.

'See you Thursday. At the party. Nine o'clock,' came back faintly.

'Guess you won't be seeing her till Thursday then mate,' Ash said. 'D'you fancy taking the Land Rover out. Go to the coast, you can have a drive?'

He unfolded his long limbs and brushed the strands of hay off his T-shirt. A stream of sunlight gilded his black hair with tips of gold. He smiled, 'You on then? I'll go and grab the keys.'

'Yeah, course.' And I followed him down the ladder into the hazy afternoon. Thursday wasn't that far away.

Later, when the afternoon had given way to a pearly soft evening, we sat on the sea wall in Seahouses and ate fish and chips from the paper.

'We haven't done this for ages,' Ash said, spearing a chip with the wooden fork, 'we used to come down here all the time.'

'We ought to do it more often. Just the two of us.'

'No women, yeah. Makes a nice change doesn't it.' He flung a bit of fish skin over the wall and immediately two gulls came screaming in, necks outstretched, beaks gaping. Between them they missed the scrap and Ash laughed as they dived down into the harbour after their meal.

'You gonna take Bethany to the party?' I asked, not looking at him.

'No.'

'I just thought you might.'

'No. I don't think it'd be her scene. Anyway Angel didn't invite her.'

'She probably wouldn't mind though. There'll be loads of people there. One more isn't going to make any difference.'

'Hey, if you want Bethany to come ask her yourself and I'll escort Angel.' He fired a bit of batter at the seagulls and this time one of them caught it and veered away, squawking in triumph.

I took a deep breath, felt something catch at the bottom of my stomach. 'Ash, you don't fancy Angel do you?' It came out too fast for me to take it back. He turned to look at me.

'No.'

'Ok then. I just thought. Only I'm going away in a couple of weeks and…'

'And you don't want me keeping your girlfriend company when you go? So, I won't. You done?' He screwed his chip paper into a ball and stuffed it into a nearby bin, wiping his hands on his shorts. I stuffed another couple of chips in my mouth and binned the paper.

Chapter Twenty-six

The music met us as soon as we turned into the driveway and we followed the pounding bass round the side of the house to the workshops. We were both in full goth gear with spiked hair and eyeliner. Mum had been very unimpressed.

We turned the corner into the courtyard and the muted grey evening burst into life with colour and light and noise. Right in the centre of the courtyard there was a massive barbecue with six foot torches burning at each side. The three stable wings were dripping with ropes of gold and pink fairy lights and there were braziers burning in the corners, sending shadows dancing wildly up the walls. Music, a heavy, driving beat, rolled towards us from the impressive sound system in one of the doorways. And everywhere people, dancing, drinking, gathering round the braziers, pushing in front of the barbecue. This was obviously not one of those parties which took forever to get started.

'They don't all live here do they?' Ash shouted above the music.

'No. There's only about ten of them here all the time. They must have invited everybody they ever knew.'

'And then some.' For a moment we stood on the edge of it all, Ash dangling a four pack from each hand, me with a couple of bottles of cider.

'Weird lot aren't they?' Ash said. I looked round. It was a bit like a colourful collision of flower children, Romany gypsies and hippies on acid, with, thankfully, a sprinkling of goth. I'd never seen so many flowery waistcoats, dreadlocks, beards and body piercings.

'I can see where Angel gets it from,' Ash said, 'where's the bar?' He shouldered his way into the throng and I followed him, keeping one eye out for Angel.

The bar was in one of the stables, a dozen big barrels packed with ice, cans and bottles. Philip was in charge and he nodded at Ash, 'Stick the booze in a barrel and take your pick. There's skiffs over there. If you want wine there's some of my stuff in the jugs by the window. Food is next door.' He nodded through an arch to the next stable. 'My stepdaughter's through there I think,' he told Ash, who nodded and raised a can of lager to him.

'Thanks. I'll go and find her,' I said pointedly, grabbing a can.

Angel was standing by a long table, which was piled with bowls of bean salad and veggie snacks, deep in conversation with a big, bearded bloke in his sixties. She had a sandwich in one hand and a bottle of beer in the other and was waving them both around animatedly as she talked. She caught sight of us and waved us over.

'Hi. Come and meet Ron. He's from our old commune in Wales. Ron, this is David and Ash.' I held my hand out but Ron just nodded and I let my hand fall back by my side.

'Ron.' Ash raised his hand in mock salute and Ron saluted him back.

'Ron's trying to lure us back to Wales. Says it's not been the same since we left,' she giggled.

'How could it be the same without you, Angel,' Ron said and leered at her.

'Philip's not going to up and leave now. Not after everything he's spent on this place. And all his plans are just coming to fruition.' She looked at Ron and he gave a brief nod. 'Doesn't mean I couldn't go back myself though. Maybe on a visit.' She looked thoughtful. 'But then you should never go back should you?' She tilted her face for him to plant a wet kiss on her beautiful cheek. 'See you later Ron.'

'See you later, sweetheart.' He grinned as Angel moved away.

We followed her out into the courtyard and Ash went to get another round of drinks. Angel sat on the edge of a stone water trough to watch the dancing and I sat as close as I could. I wanted to put my arm round her but the back of the trough got in the way so instead I took her hand. She looked at me with the ghost of a smile and I started stroking the palm of her hand, running my fingertips along her wrist and then I lifted her hand and pressed it to my lips. She didn't respond and I let our joined hands fall back into her lap. Above the courtyard the moon was full and heavy, pregnant with old gold light.

On the makeshift dance floor, the dancing was growing wilder. Music I didn't recognise swooped and wheeled around the stable block, up into the trees and down onto the moon washed cobbles. Arms snaked into the air, braids flashed with beads and bodies pulsed in time with the rhythms, at once ancient and fresh. The flames from the brazier cast demonic shadows on the whitewashed walls and sexual energy throbbed through the night. I moved closer to Angel as we watched figures merging then slipping into the shadows. I wanted to touch her, to pull her into my arms and kiss her with all the passion of the night but instead I took the joint she offered and let her light it from a tiny, emerald lighter. Our smoke mingled and went to meet the smoke from the fires, spiralling into the sky.

Ash reappeared. His eyes were glittering so I knew he'd been drinking but he hadn't brought any back with him.

'I thought you were getting the drinks in,' I said.

'Was I? Yeah I probably was. Sorry, I got distracted.' He smiled and took a joint from Angel. 'Good party this. Could do with a beer though, mate.'

'Don't look at me. You were supposed to be getting them in.' I didn't want to get annoyed. It wasn't cool.

'Yeah, like I said, I got distracted. Philip had this carrot whisky he'd distilled. Couldn't say no, could I? Not to Angel's dad.'

'Stepdad. Go and get us some cans David. Ash is hopeless. You can't trust him with anything.' She squeezed my hand and smiled like she meant it.

'I suppose so. But then you're going to dance with me.'

'Of course. I've been waiting for you to ask.' And her laughter followed me across the courtyard.

By the time I struggled out of the crush with six cans, they were dancing. I stopped dead, my hands falling to my sides, cans dangling, and watched. Of course Ash was a good dancer. He bloody would be, but I'd never seen Angel dance. Arms raised she swayed like a flower in the breeze and Ash moved round her, not touching but inhabiting the same space. She said something and he bent closer to hear, his face against her hair. They broke away, both of them laughing and continued the dance.

I stomped back to the trough and dumped the cans in the water to keep cool. I folded my arms and waited for them to come back. 'It's fine,' I told myself. 'You've danced with Celia loads of times and Ash never minded. They're friends for God's sake.'

And then they came back and they were both relaxed and chatty and I smiled like everything was fine. And after a few minutes and some beer, everything was fine. Angel dragged me off to dance and I acted like I was reluctant, waving over my shoulder to Ash and he just watched with his eyes narrowed and his can raised.

Dancing with Angel in the moonlight was like being back in the studio that first time. Her hair was full of incense and she held me close and whispered wicked things about the other dancers in my ear. Her hips moved against mine and I wondered when we could be alone, if any of the stables were empty. I bent forward to kiss her but like a shadow she slipped out of my arms and I found myself dancing with a pretty hippy girl with pre-

Raphaelite curls. Angel waved at me over Ron's shoulder. Then we were caught up in a spiral dance, everyone dancing, turning, corkscrewing into the centre of the circle, then out again, pattern forming from chaos. Now and then I caught a glimpse of Ash. He wasn't dancing. Instead he leaned against the wall, smoking joint after joint.

The dance broke apart with a final throb of the drums and I found Angel beside me, both of us out of breath, laughing, exhilarated. I grabbed her shoulders and pulled her towards me. I kissed her hard and felt her arms come round my neck as she kissed me back. We broke briefly apart and as I went to kiss her again I saw Ash grind out his joint under his heel and turn away.

People started drifting inside and we followed. The place had been cleared out for the night and there were rugs and cushions scattered around the floor. We crashed by a wall and picked at tofu pies and veggie sausages from the barbecue. The music had mellowed and I felt stoned. I asked Angel where the toilets were and she pointed me off towards a dark corner. I picked my way across the room, stepping between clinched couples and huddled groups. The air was thick with smoke from candles, cannabis and tobacco. In the tiny toilet block a girl and a bloke were snorting coke from a silver shard of mirror. They didn't look up when I walked in but I kept my eyes averted.

On the way back I passed a couple having sex on a rug. OK, now I was shocked. The atmosphere seemed heavier, darker, more out of control. I thought about leaving. But would Ash come with me?

When I got back, they'd been joined by Ron and the wind painter, Willow.

'Hi, David.' Why did Willow unnerve me so much? It wasn't like she was particularly pretty. Not as pretty as Angel. Ash was propped up on one elbow, staring at Angel. His face seemed closed, hard. Angel offered me a tablet. A little purple pill. I looked at it, bright in the centre of her palm. I had no idea what it was. I didn't want to know. I was feeling very tired and very old and very young all at the same time.

'Go on. We've all had one. It's only phet.'

'Has he had one?' I nodded towards Ash.

'Yeah, course he has.'

'Probably why he looks so bloody vacant then. Ash, mate, I was thinking of going,' I said.

'And I was thinking of staying,' he replied.

'Do you know what you're doing?' I asked.

'Haven't got a fucking clue mate.' And I knew he meant more than just tonight.

'But if you're going to spoil things you might as well piss off home like a good boy. Leave me to it,' he said. I stared at him. But it wasn't Ash. My Ash was a long way off. I turned to Angel. She wasn't glazed or vacant. In fact she just looked amused. She held out the tablet again.

'Join us?'

If she'd said please I might have done it, for her. But she didn't. And I didn't.

I stayed for a bit, on the edge of the group, watching their eyes glitter, their hand gestures become wilder, their speech less coherent. Then Willow and Ron went to dance and Ash held out his hand to Angel.

'Come and dance with me.' Like I wasn't there. And she gave me the tiniest glance, shrugged and took his hand. I followed them and watch them glide out onto the dance floor, where she moved into his arms like she was going home. I watched for a minute longer, before I walked out into the night. Just long enough to see him bend his head and her lift her face to him as they kissed. Then I was outside and only half way across the courtyard before I was throwing up on the cobbles, sick to the heart at what they'd done.

Chapter Twenty-seven

I was still staggering down the long driveway, wiping away vomit with the back of my hand when I heard the sirens. Spiralling through the night they were getting closer and then the whole driveway was swept clean by headlights. I dived for the bushes as four police cars, blue lights swirling, swept past, towards the Hall. I lurked in the shadows, torn between wanting to see what was happening and not really giving a damn. The effects of drink, drugs and a broken heart won out and after a last glance towards the Hall, still illuminated by the headlights, I trudged home.

Morning inevitably arrived and I was hung over and miserable. I couldn't get out of bed. Apart from the usual dust dry mouth and shouting headache, I felt like I'd swallowed a big, heavy stone. There was no point getting up, no point opening the curtains; I was going to spend eternity in this bedroom, in this bed, because nothing mattered any more. Present and future were a grey, formless void.

Mum appeared out of the void. I pulled the duvet away from my face and mouthed, 'go away.' She knew better than to disturb me after a heavy night. Usually she left it till at least 11am before she started hoovering right outside my room. If I wasn't out by noon she might stick her head round the door, 'just checking you're still breathing.'

Not this morning. The illuminated dial by my bed told me it was only 9am and she was here tugging back the curtains.

I tried to lift my head, 'Mum. Please go away.' Couldn't she see I needed to be left alone to waste away. She was my mother, she should sense these things.

She sat down on the edge of the bed and fixed me with a look. She was very serious this morning, her lips compressed, her cheeks a bit flushed, as though she were angry and trying not to show it.

'What?' I asked.

'I want to know exactly what went on last night.'

I groaned, 'Oh, Mum, you really don't. I just had a heavy night.'

'There was a police raid at the Hall. They were after drugs. And you were there. So what happened?' I closed my eyes and took a deep breath. What the hell was I going to say. When I opened my eyes, Dad was standing by the window, fiddling with the edge of the curtain.

'David, we need to know what happened at the Hall. Were you there when the police came? Were there drugs there?'

'And were you taking them?' Mum's voice became shrill and I winced.

'We need to know, David,' Dad sounded so disappointed, 'whatever happened.'

'Nothing did happen. Can't we talk about this later.' I tried to pull the covers over my head but Mum yanked them out of my hands.

'No we can't. For all we know the police are going to be hammering at that door any minute and dragging you off to court. So, no, we can't talk about it later.' Alarmingly she was about to cry.

I sat up and put my arm round her, 'No-one's going to come and take me anywhere because I haven't done anything. You know I don't take drugs.' I crossed the fingers of my other hand firmly under the duvet.

'Why don't you wear pyjamas?' Mum pulled away and looked round for my dressing gown.

'But were you there when the police came?' Dad insisted. If he wasn't careful he was going to pull the curtain off the rail.

'No. I'd left by then. I was walking home when I heard the sirens. That's all. You obviously know more about it than me.'

I pulled my dressing gown round me and sat on the edge of the bed. Mum took my hand and looked into my face, 'Were there drugs there? Did you see anything.'

I swallowed, 'Yes. There were people smoking pot. I wasn't one of them. If there was any harder stuff there, I didn't see it. Ok?'

They exchanged glances.

'Don't you believe me? Do you want me to take a drugs test or something?' I looked affronted. Please don't let them want me to take a drugs test.

'Of course we believe you son.' Dad came and stood

beside me. 'But you've got to understand how we felt. A drugs raid and our son in the middle of it. It's not what we expect.' He looked old and worried and I hated that Angel had done that.

'I don't take drugs Dad. You know me better than that. I know I drink too much sometimes but that's all. And I won't be going to the Hall again, if that's any consolation.' It wasn't so hard to say it.

'Angel?' Dad asked.

'Angel. And I'm not talking about it.' I started to climb back into bed. 'I've got a really bad headache. Mum, would you get me some Paracetamol please. And maybe a nice cup of tea.' I sank back into the pillows and Mum got up and started straightening the covers.

'Tea, tablets. Do you want any toast?'

'No thank you, not just now,' I murmured. 'Maybe later.' She hurried out, pleased to have something to do. I looked at my dad.

'I'm sorry I worried you, Dad.'

'It's alright. We should have had more faith in you.' He gave me a penetrating look and I wasn't sure that I'd convinced him. 'It won't be a bad thing to keep away from the Hall though. There's something not right there. I've always thought so.' He shook his head and I closed my eyes before he could say anything else.

The raid was a waste of time. I knew it would be. What did the police think they were going to achieve, arriving with sirens shrieking? I imagined the panic that would have set in when they were first heard in the workshops though. The party would have broken up in a split second. The word in the village was that the police had got a tip off and searched the Hall first. By the time they got to the workshops all they found were a few sleepy people clearing up after a get together. They still wouldn't have had much time to get rid of the drugs and I wondered where they'd stashed them all. The police didn't find a thing. I'd have found that suspicious enough – all those hippies and not a single joint? But the police left and for now it was end of story.

Except it wasn't. Angel rang me in the afternoon. She never rang me and I wished she'd stuck to form. I had nothing to say to her.

'David?'

'Yeah.'

'It's Angel.'

'I know.'

'I think we need to talk, don't you?'

'That depends on what you have to say.'

'I think what you have to say is more important.'

'Whatever.'

I said she could come round. She could try to explain.

'Ok. What the fuck were you doing, running to the police?' She was only just through the door and Mum and Dad were in the kitchen. I shushed her and pointed up the stairs. She glared but marched up to my bedroom. I followed, brain in overdrive. Running to the police? Me? She thought I'd grassed them up?

She sat down on the bed, her denim mini dress riding

right up her thighs. I sat at my desk, across the room from her. I didn't trust myself any closer.

'So?' She tilted her head on one side and waited. 'What did you run to the police for?'

'I didn't. What did you kiss Ash for?'

'What's that got to do with it?'

'Everything.'

'Oh, so you grassed us up 'cos I kissed Ash? Very mature,' she sneered.

'I didn't grass you up! If you're stupid enough to take that stuff, that's your problem. Don't blame me if you get caught.' We both stood up, tried to stare each other down.

'We didn't get caught did we?'

'You got caught with Ash.'

'Oh back to that.' She turned away. 'Really, what's the big deal?'

'The big deal is you were with me and you kissed him.'

'Oh David,' she sighed, 'you don't understand?' Then she came across the room. She stood very close and ran her fingers across the back of my neck. I swallowed hard.

'I kissed Ash because we both wanted to. If you remember all you wanted to do was go home. But that was last night.' She slipped her fingers inside the neck of my T-shirt. Then she bent down like she was going to kiss me and I shoved her away, hard.

'Get off,' I stood up as she staggered sideways, her eyes dark with anger.

'What the fuck do you think you're doing?' she said.

'Did you sleep with him?' And when she didn't reply, 'Did you?'

'Yeah,' she said quietly and my ears started fizzing so I had to shake my head. She was supposed to deny it. She was still talking and I struggled to focus on the words, through the noise in my head.

'Like I said, it just happened. I was in the moment. But it didn't mean anything.' I could believe that.

'Like I suppose it never meant anything with me all those times?' I said.

'What was it supposed to mean David?' She stepped towards me but I stepped back.

'Oh I don't know. Commitment, fidelity, love maybe?' I struggled to keep my voice down. I didn't want Mum barging in here.

'Love? Commitment? God, David, we were having some fun, not planning a bloody wedding. What do you want to make it so serious for?'

'Because it is serious. I loved you. I thought you felt the same but no, you were just lusting after Ash.'

She shook her head, 'I like you David. I like you a lot.'

'Yeah, and you like Ash. And you probably like old Ron from Wales and half a dozen of the other blokes from the Hall.'

'And if I do? What's that got to do with you?' Her grey eyes were like flint chips.

'Nothing apparently. You shag my best friend and it's nothing to do with me. Fucking great.' My voice cracked and I sat down on the bed.

She sat down next to me, her thigh tight against mine,

but all I could think was that Ash had touched her there.

'You've made up your mind then,' she said.

'I guess you made it for me,' but then she leaned forward and kissed me. Her lips melted into mine and I slipped my hand behind her head and pulled her to me, hard. Ash had kissed her like this. I pulled away.

'What about Ash?'

She shrugged and wouldn't meet my eye.

'You'd carry on seeing him wouldn't you?'

'Probably. You always shared Celia, I didn't think you'd mind sharing me.' Her lips twisted in a smile.

'Get out,' I said quietly.

She didn't move.

'Get out Angel. Just get the fuck out.'

She stayed for a second or two and I fixed my eyes on the tree outside the window. Then she got up and I heard the door close behind her with a little click. I carried on staring out of the window but I couldn't see a thing.

The next couple of days made no impression. They came and they went. I slept, listened to depressing music and refused to eat. Even sunk in my misery I realised I'd become a stereotype. But what the hell. I was 18. My heart was broken. What else was I supposed to do. Stereotypes are only stereotypes because they are true.

I wanted to kill Ash. It was his fault. He always got what he wanted, who he wanted and no-one ever argued with him. So, his dad made him work at the boatyard but in exchange he got well paid, had the use of the Land Rover, the boats. Now he'd taken Angel and he'd expect me to let it happen. I might not be able to get her back, might not want her back, but he had to pay for it. I fantasised about a tragic car crash, a boating accident, a fatal overdose. More realistically I started to plan an ambush. I could wait for him in the morning, jump him getting into the Land Rover, when he was all hungover. Or I'd wait for him coming back, pissed, from the pub. I was angry but not enough to forget that he'd crucify me in a straight fight. I brooded and kicked furniture and wished it was Ash.

Mum ordered Dad to take me to the pub. I overheard her.

'Just get him out of the house will you. I can't take another night of that awful music and if he kicks his desk again it'll collapse. Get him drunk if you have to, just make him snap out of it.' I smiled for the first time in a week.

So we went down The Plough. I wondered if Derek would remember I was banned, but if he did he didn't say anything. Dad was a restful companion. He didn't try to say the right thing all the time. He was best at saying nothing at all. I could sit with Dad over a couple of pints for ages without talking and it would feel ok.

He didn't try to cheer me up. He just plonked a pint in front of me, 'I'm sorry it didn't work out with Angel, son. She wouldn't have been my choice but I know how you felt about her.'

'Yeah, well, we all make mistakes.' I tried a bitter laugh.

'I'm a good listener but you're not going to talk to your dad are you?' he smiled as I slowly shook my head. 'At least you've got Ashley for that.'

'Ash?' I looked up with a start but he didn't know anything, thought me and Ash were still best mates. Probably didn't expect my best mate to be screwing my girlfriend. Funny that. I didn't disabuse him

So, we talked about me leaving for Uni until it was time to walk home, through the dusty heat. I looked up at the royal blue sky and the stars winking back at me without a scrap of cloud to cloak them. It hadn't rained for far too long.

As we came up to our gate, Dad stopped abruptly, so abruptly I nearly fell over him, as he peered into the shadows of the Old Vicarage. I followed his gaze and noticed that the light was on in Ash's bedroom. Nothing unusual there. Then I saw a darker patch of shadow apparently struggling in a flowerbed at the base of the house.

'Burglars?' said Dad, one hand on the gate.

I heard a low giggle from the darkness and Ash's head appeared at his window. My heart skipped. Then the struggling shadow resolved itself into Angel, climbing up the trellis to the open window and bitterness clogged the back of my throat.

'Not burglars Dad,' I said and pushed our garden gate open.

'So that's how it is,' he said and followed me inside.

I couldn't do this on my own anymore. Dad might sympathise but he wouldn't tell me how to kick Ash's head in; wouldn't listen to a stream of expletives as I summed up how I felt. I needed a best friend. In the absence of Ash I prayed for Celia to come home.

Chapter Twenty-eight

Celia called me. She'd been home a day and sounded very upbeat.

'You going to bring me up to date then? Fill me in on all the gossip?' She didn't mention Ash but it was what she meant and now I had the chance, I didn't know what to say. I couldn't just blurt it out. 'Oh yes, Ash is fine but he's screwing Angel now. How do I feel about it? Pretty pissed considering.' Instead I said I'd go round.

Celia met me with a smile and a kiss on the cheek and I resisted the urge to hug her and bury my face in her long hair. She'd arranged deckchairs under a stripy umbrella in the back garden. She poured us both beers, the cans still frosted from the fridge and tipped some crisps into a white bowl. I liked going to Celia's house, she made me feel properly welcome.

I could have sat in her garden all afternoon, drinking beer and watching the bees flit in and out of the flowers on the patio. I half closed my eyes and let the sun lap against my legs whilst my face was cool in the shade. After a bit though she sat up and asked how Ash was and there was no getting away from it. I told her everything, just as it had happened; the cannabis, getting thrown out of The

Plough, the party, the scene with Angel, then I braced myself for her reaction. I'd come prepared with a pocket full of tissues. After the tears she'd be angry and I was looking forward to that bit. I had plenty of anger of my own to share.

Celia let me down. She listened without interrupting once, then sat back and took a swig of her drink, 'I told you she'd get him didn't I?'

I stared and she laughed at me.

'Did you want me to break down and sob and say I can't live without him?'

I shrugged in a 'well some reaction would have been good' way.

'I've done with crying and begging. I tried it on Holy Island and look how well that went.' I had a flashing memory of a sobbing Celia, clinging to Ash on Cuthbert's Isle.

'After Holy Island I knew she'd got her claws into him. Well, now he's getting what he thinks he wants, we'll have to see how long it lasts.' She put her glass down on the table, forming a puddle of condensation.

'D'you want another beer,' she offered.

I shook my head. I was confused. She wasn't angry, or bitter.

'But don't you hate them?' I asked.

She reached out and plucked some dead petals from the geranium by her chair and looked thoughtful, 'I don't hate them, no. I mean I kind of hate Angel but it's more I despise her. She's not worth the energy it'd take to hate her.'

Probably why I was so tired all the time.

'But of course I don't hate Ash.' And her face lit up, like it used to when Ash walked in or when he whispered in her ear. It was scary.

'You don't still love him? After what he's done?' I couldn't help my voice rising.

'Of course I love him. I'll always love him.' She was positively glowing now. 'What's happening now, it's nothing. I've had loads of time to think about it. Ash has had a really bad time.' I raised my eyebrows. 'He messed up his exams, so he can't come to Uni. And he always struggled with the no sex thing. Well, now he can have all the sex he wants, with Angel.' I winced but she didn't notice. 'She'll screw him, then she'll dump him and I'll be there waiting. Me and Ash are too strong to be finished by someone like her.'

She smiled at me, all serene and accepting and I wanted to say it doesn't look like that from here. I didn't get it. Maybe she was being mature, being a Christian, knowing how to forgive. Maybe she was just obsessed. Either way it wasn't right. She ought to hate them, the way I did. I wanted them to get hurt. Really, badly, hurt.

* * *

I waited for Ash behind the Landrover. It was Friday, so I knew he'd be going to the boatyard, however late a night he'd had. His dad would kill him otherwise. I'd spent half the night staring across at the Old Vicarage, straining to catch a glimpse of Angel. About 2am Ash had let her out of the front door. She was in bare feet and she slipped her

179

shoes on, holding onto Ash's arm to balance. I spent those early hours of the morning twisting it round in my head. I didn't want Angel back but I couldn't just hand her to him on a plate.

So, I crouched behind the Landrover, waiting for my moment. Surprise attack, rely on speed and his reluctance to hurt me. He came round the side of the house rubbing his head like he always did when he hadn't had enough sleep. Thinking about why he hadn't slept made me clench my fists and I took a few deep breaths. I had to stay in control. As he came level with the Landrover I could see he hadn't shaved and there were purple shadows under his eyes. Too much eyeliner or else being with Angel wasn't doing him much good. He bent to put the key in the door. There was a dodgy lock and I'd get my chance while he was fiddling with that. I just needed to move quickly and hit him hard, first time. I stepped out from behind the car, arm swinging, one step, two, he looked up, I hesitated and my momentum was gone. I stopped, fist raised, expecting him to swing at me. Instead he took a step away from the car.

'David.'

'You enjoy screwing my girlfriend?' I asked.

'Your girlfriend?' He raised his eyebrows and I swung at him. I don't know if I connected because the next thing he'd landed a fist in my face. As I staggered back he jabbed his knee into my groin and I went down. His foot went back like he was going to kick me and I reflexed into a ball, hands over my head.

Then I heard the door open, the engine start and a clatter of gravel as he pulled away.

Part Four

Samhain

Chapter Twenty-nine

Whatever I felt about Ash and Angel, I had to get ready to go away. October was about to start and with it my life at University. It was strange, packing up my life. I'd be coming home for holidays and maybe weekends but it felt like I was leaving home for good. I couldn't ever see me living here again full time. Not now. I was scared, leaving my life behind, but impatient as well. I couldn't wait to get back to the city, find a new me in its anonymity. I packed my black clothes, confident I wouldn't be the only goth on campus. I stacked my CDs in a box and unplugged my stereo, then plugged it in again because I couldn't pack without music. Mum had bought me a kettle and a mug tree with matching mugs. It was hideous but I let her pack it and vowed I'd shop for cooler mugs, first chance I got. Me leaving home for the first time was a bigger thing for her than it was for me.

The day before I left I went to the local shop to get a final few things. Mum had already stacked two cardboard boxes with every food that could be tinned; bumper jars of Fairtrade coffee and enough pasta and rice to last me till graduation but I still needed razors, aspirin and for some reason black cotton which she swore I couldn't do without. The shop was full. Either paying-the-papers-day or something was going on. I got some questioning looks from a couple of the customers, then it was my turn to be served and Jilly stage whispered across the counter.

'Suppose you know all about them getting arrested then?'

'About who getting arrested?' I leaned in.

'Those two from the Hall? Thought you'd know more than me, going out with the daughter and all.'

'Yeah well I don't. So tell me.'

'Not split up, have you?' When I didn't reply, 'Well two of them artists got arrested in Alnwick last night. Apparently they were selling drugs and they've been in court this morning.'

'Yeah?' I wasn't surprised. 'Do you know who they were?'

'No. One of my customers has a brother at the court. He couldn't tell her the names, but he said one was a big bloke with a beard and the other was a woman.'

Sounded like big Ron. That was a bitter blow. I could only hope the other one was Angel.

After weeks of sun, the heat finally fused the atmosphere and the weather broke on my last night at home. The storm erupted somewhere out at sea and tore inland, lashing the village. I watched from my window, as for hours great jagged shards of lightning jabbed blue fingers into the earth and I waited for the crack of thunder. The hairs on my neck crept with static and when the rain finally came I leaned out of the window, my face tilted to the heavens until my T-shirt was soaked flat to my body.

The next day, as I helped Dad load the car, I saw the storm had brought down a huge tree in the Hall grounds. It had fallen across the wall, right where the side gate was, and half across our lane. Until the council bothered to send out a team to shift it, Ash and Angel were going to have to find themselves another route.

As if I'd summoned him by my thoughts, Ash appeared, loping across the grass between the two houses. He looked like he was coming my way, so I ducked under the boot of the car with a box of books. When I looked up he was standing by the gate. He hadn't shaved again. I walked straight past him, back into the house to collect another box. Dad passed me, arms filled with my duvet and went to the car.

'Morning Mr Wilson,' Ash said. Since when had he been so polite?

'Ashley.' Dad dumped the duvet on the back seat and came back in without so much as glancing at Ash. I was proud of him. I thought Ash would go away then, but when I came out again he was still there, leaning against the car. He looked really rough, more than hung over. Probably on something. I sighed and went over, 'What? Come to give me another kicking.'

'No.' He looked surprised. 'That shouldn't have happened. I came to wish you luck.' He actually smiled at me.

'You are kidding?'

'No. I wish I was coming with you.' He looked like he meant it and I got the feeling that he wanted to say something else, something that might change things.

185

'Well, I'm fucking glad you're not.' I threw the box into the car and went back inside. When I looked again he'd gone.

We got to the accommodation block in the late afternoon and I let Mum and Dad help carry everything up to my second floor room. Although Mum wanted to stay and unpack all my boxes, I insisted that they left, to drive home in time for dinner. I didn't want her fussing around. Unpacking and finding somewhere for all my stuff would give me something to do while I adjusted to my new home. I waved them off, ignoring Mum's wobbling lip and the lump in my own throat, and went to survey my room.

I was going to be living in a box. One box among many identical boxes in the huge accommodation block, Freeman's Square, half a mile from the main campus. I had a desk, a chair, a bed, wardrobe and a sink in one corner. There was a shared bathroom down the corridor and a kitchen, where I'd have my own lockable cupboard and some space in the fridge. A notice on the front of the fridge advised everyone to label their food and warned thieves to keep off Angie's cheese.

I'd passed a few other students on the stairs, while I was bringing my stuff up and we'd exchanged nods and tentative smiles. Now I could hear movement in some of the other six rooms on my floor but there was no-one about when I stuck my head into the corridor. I boiled the kettle in the corner of my room and unhooked a mug from Mum's mug tree. I could have another five drinks before I needed to wash up.

That first night I had a choice of places to go. The noticeboards in the block were covered with posters advertising start of term events and there were half a dozen flyers under my door, requesting my presence in venues around the city. I didn't want to go to any of them. Not to the big party at the Student's Union with a halfway decent band, or to the Cultural Society's Drumming Fest or anywhere else. I wanted to stay in my room and play depressing music and think about what Ash and Angel were doing. In other words exactly what they would expect me to do. So I'd have to go out.

Whilst burning cheese on toast in the kitchen, I met Craig from Leeds, who had the room two down from mine and he asked if I was going to the gig in Freeman's Square bar. It was close by, there was no entrance charge, so I said yes.

As we walked across the grassy communal 'square' I smelled autumn through the dark. Ash and Celia had always mocked me for my love of the season of decay.

'Going back to school, dark nights, everything dying. What's there to like?' Ash, devotee of summer, used to say.

Even Celia thought autumn was depressing. She liked the promise of spring. But I loved autumn, nothing was better than a sudden sunny day at the end of September. The earth was quiet, replete after harvest, there was the sense of rest and peace and accomplishment. The world was older, wiser, kinder in autumn. I felt my place more assured, could see where I stood. Winter was too forbidding, spring unsettling and summer had burned me up.

Now, walking across the square, I breathed in the familiar scents of fallen leaves and turned earth and realised I could find my place here as well as in the village. The wheel of the year would keep turning, and me with it, and as the year changed so I could change. Autumn here was different from autumn at home, the fallen leaves from the bordering sycamores thicker on the ground; the scent of earth not so strong; the dark filtered through streetlights. And I could be different here. I could be anyone I wanted. Without Ash, David could remake himself.

At least half the students in the bar were dressed in black. It was almost a disappointment, fitting in so well. I bought Craig a pint at the corner bar and was stunned at how cheap it was. Ash would be in heaven. But Ash wasn't here.

The room was big, dipped in darkness with groups of chairs around the walls, a space for dancing in the middle and a small stage at the far end. Craig recognised someone he knew and I followed him over to a couple of spare seats in a big group of people. I found myself sitting next to a very small girl in black, with bushy brown hair. She turned to me straight away, pushing her hair off her face. She had thick black eyeliner rimming her blue eyes and half a dozen hooped silver earrings marching up the edge of her ear.

'Hi, I'm Lorna.' She had a strange, heavy accent. 'Do you want to buy me another drink?' She waved an empty glass at me. 'I'm not pissed, I just want a drink.' She didn't sound at all pissed and I took her glass and waited for her order.

'Southern Comfort and Appletise please.' I had to ask her twice but she seemed clear and the student barman didn't hesitate but poured Southern Comfort from the optic and handed me a bottle of Appletise. I shrugged and took it back to Lorna, who greeted me, or the drink, with delight.

The group were mainly Freshers. They came from all over the place – Leeds, Leicester, Mansfield, Hong Kong, the Orkneys. I was the only one who lived within a couple of hours drive and I felt a bit parochial.

Lorna told me she'd had to set off two days ago to get here from the Orkneys, relying on boats, trains and buses. She didn't care at all about being so far from home. She'd been a boarder at her school since she was eleven because her family lived too far out of town for her to travel every day. She wished she'd gone further south, 'as far away from the Orkneys as possible' but this had been a good course and she'd got a place. She was studying languages. I tried to imagine how Italian would sound in her Orkadian accent.

After a bit the band came on, a student band called the Myth Surrounding Eve, and they were ok. They only did covers but it was Indie stuff I liked and they played enthusiastically. I bought Lorna another drink, then she went to get a round in. The room was filling up by then and she was gone a while. I thought she might have gone home, but then she appeared, forcing her way through the crowd, clutching a couple of bottles of Appletise and the whole bottle of Southern Comfort.

'Save going back to the bar. You'll have to have some of this if you want another drink.' I grinned at her and acknowledged Craig's thumbs up.

The room was throbbing with music and dancing. I finished my pint and started Lorna's Southern Comfort, disliking the sweetness in my throat but loving the warm hit in my belly and the way Lorna looked at me over the rim of the bottle. We started kissing and she tasted of apples and fire. Her lips moved hungrily under mine and I fastened my hands in her hair and pulled her against me. I don't know who made the first move to go but then we were out in the night air and I was kissing her against the wall. She pushed her hands up under my T-shirt and I felt for her breasts.

'Your room.' She whispered against my ear. 'You have got condoms?'

I froze and she laughed and said, 'Good job I have then.'

Next morning I daren't open my eyes. Either she'd be gone or she'd still be in my bed and it would be awkward and difficult. I was wrong with both guesses. When I forced my eyes open and rolled over, Lorna was sitting on the window sill, fully dressed and drinking from one of my mugs.

'Morning. Can I get you a coffee? Wake you up a bit?'

'Yeah, alright.' I yawned and reached for the sheet to cover myself, before I got out of bed.

'I wouldn't bother with that, I saw it all last night,' she said, as she poured boiling water into a mug. Mum would be pleased they were getting used so soon.

While I got dressed, pretending I didn't mind her watching, Lorna talked. She told me about her room, on the far side of the Square, her floormates; what parties she was going to; which bands were supposed to be cool; when the first students union meeting was. She was a walking guidebook to student life.

'Anyway,' she swung down from the window sill, 'I better be off now. I haven't unpacked properly and there's a beer festival in one of the Halls of Residence later. You going?'

I shrugged. I was supposed to be meeting Celia.

'I might see you there. If not catch up some time, yeah?' When she was halfway through the door she turned, 'It was good last night. Thanks. I like it like this, no strings, no dramas.' I'd heard that before but now it was what I wanted.

When I heard her footsteps receding down the corridor, I licked the tip of my forefinger and inscribed a number one in the air.

Chapter Thirty

I caught a bus across town to Celia's shared house. Her term had started a couple of weeks before mine and she'd sent me a carefully drawn map, with bus routes marked in red and a big blue arrow pointing to, 'Eastlands – Celia lives here.'

It was raining when I walked up the path and rang the bell. No-one came for ages and I hadn't brought an umbrella. I turned my coat collar up and kept my finger on the bell. It was a big red brick house, probably owned by a doctor or a solicitor when it was built in the 19th century, and now condemned to house an ever changing population of students.

I was crouching down to shout through the letterbox when someone tapped me on the shoulder. I stood up too abruptly and the world swam as I tried to focus on the tall girl in glasses.

'The bell doesn't work, as you've probably gathered. Who are you looking for?'

When I told her she raised her eyebrows, 'Celia? The girl who doesn't want to be here.' She stood aside to let me into the entrance hall and pointed me up the wide flight of stairs, 'Room 10. Up the stairs, end of the corridor, up the second flight and she's the third door along. See if you can convince her to come out now and then.' The girl disappeared into a room at the front of the house and I went on up the stairs.

It must have been wonderful to live here in the 1800s. Sweeping stairs, ornate banister, wide landings and high ceilings. I thought of my box in the Square.

I knocked and Celia yelled, 'come in,' flinging the door open at the same time so that we almost collided and instead ended up in a big hug. I wrapped my arms round her and breathed in the fresh shampoo scent of her hair. For the first time ever I didn't feel turned on. I was startled and pulled away, 'Show me round then.'

She smiled and waved her hand to encompass the room, 'My kingdom, such as it is. I'm a freshman so I get the servants quarters up here. Next year I'll get a room on the first floor, with more space and a sink and if I stay till the third year I might get one of the rooms on the ground floor. They're massive. Very strict pecking order here.' She didn't seem to mind.

'Oh we're very egalitarian in my place.' I told her. 'We all have exactly the same amount of floor space, bit like battery hens.' We laughed.

Her room was small but nice. There was a big window with a low, wide windowsill where you could sit and look out across the roof tops to the city. The room had been freshly painted and there was a newish desk and a bookcase, which Celia had already filled.

'They think you're unsociable downstairs.' I told her. She looked a bit surprised.

'Do they? Do you want a coffee?'

I shook my head, 'I thought we could have a walk, find a pub or something.'

'You're as bad as Ash.' She was smiling but I winced.

'What? I can say his name you know.'

'Well, I'd rather you didn't.'

'Don't be so pathetic.' She glared and the silence grew uncomfortable.

'Go on, make me a coffee then.' I gave in.

'Ok, but I'll have to get the milk from the kitchen downstairs. When it gets cold I'll stick a carton on the windowsill outside, save running up and down. We really need a fridge on this floor.'

While she was gone I looked through the books on her shelves. Mostly art books, some poetry but no novels and none of her favourite Christian books.

'God upset you has He?' I asked when she came back, 'Only I notice you haven't brought Him along.'

'No, I haven't brought any of my best books.' She handed me a mug with a milky scum on the top and sat down on the bed.

'I think the milk's going off a bit. Drink it fast and you won't notice.'

I grimaced. 'Nice. Why haven't you brought your books? They won't get nicked. Thieves are not that literate you know. They only want stereos and cash.'

'I know. I haven't brought them 'cos I won't be here that much to read them will I?'

'Won't you?'

'Well no. We'll not be here many weekends will we?'

'Won't we?'

She stared at me. 'No, we'll be going home. To the village.'

'Why?'

'To keep an eye on Ash. Make sure he's OK with Angel.'

She was talking very slowly, as if I was very stupid. I answered in kind, 'I really don't care whether he's alright with Angel or not. I'd rather he wasn't actually. Can we talk about something else. I met this girl last night.'

'That's nice.'

'She's called Lorna. She stayed the night but it's nothing serious, just casual you know.'

Why did I think that was a good thing to say to Celia?

'I don't know. I don't do casual. And I didn't think you did. Angel wanted to be casual and you didn't like that.'

'That was different. She wanted to carry on screwing me and Ash as well.'

'And now you're going to screw this Lorna and anyone else who comes along?'

'I might do. But that's different.'

'Why different?'

'I don't love Lorna.'

There was silence. I drained my mug and pushed it across the desk. Celia picked it up and put it with hers, on the windowsill, 'I'm going home on Friday. I need to know Ash is alright, to be closer to him. Meet me at the station at 5pm?'

I shook my head.

'If you're not coming I'll ring you when I get back, tell you how things are.'

'And if I don't want to know?'

'I'll ring you anyway. I know you still care about him.'

'I'm so past caring you wouldn't believe me, but do what you want.' I kicked at a thin patch in the carpet.

'I will. Now, do you want that drink? There's an OK pub round the corner. Let's show that lot downstairs I'm not an actual recluse.' Celia grabbed her black coat from behind the door and I stood up to follow her.

'I really don't care any more.' I said.

'Ok,' she said, slotting her arm through mine, 'so tell me about Lorna.'

Chapter Thirty-one

I'd always planned to work hard at University. My parents were paying a lot for me to be there and anyway I wanted a decent job when I left. At school I'd been a pretty good student and even having Ash as best mate hadn't stopped me putting the hours in. I think it helped actually. It was good to feel superior about something. Now I was at Uni though, it was different. No Ash to compare myself to, no Celia to gently remind me when coursework was due. Now I could do what I wanted, turn up to lectures or not, fail or not, and no witnesses. It was exhilarating and I got an idea of what it must be like to be Ash. Like being on the edge of a precipice and knowing you could choose to stay on firm ground or else launch yourself into the unknown and see how you landed. But then Ash had always known he'd have a soft landing, with his family and Celia to pick him up.

I wasn't going to ditch work. I just liked knowing that I could. I skipped some of the early morning lectures and borrowed the notes from Chi, a Malaysian girl on my landing. I tried to sit next to her in lectures as well, so I could copy over her shoulder.

The trouble was there were so many parties and gigs to go to and I began to realise how starved we'd been in the village. I filled my 'Indie Chicks' calendar with the dates of all the bands I wanted to see that first term. Then there were the parties - Hall parties, block parties, room parties. I went to one every night in my first week and the more I went the more I seemed to get invited.

Being drinking buddies with Ash for three years was excellent preparation for student life, or at least the kind of student life I chose. When you're pissed you don't care much what you're saying or what's being said to you, so I was never stuck for conversation. Celia had always hated it when me and Ash were drunk and Angel just thought it was funny. Girls here found it attractive. I was never completely out of it drunk, just enough to make me a bit louder, a bit more opinionated, a bit more like Ash. The girls loved it. The blokes didn't seem to mind either.

Lorna was at a lot of the parties. We got the bus together to gigs and walked the three miles home when we missed the last one. We slept together half a dozen times in the first couple of weeks of term. I started looking out for her when I walked into a room. I knew it was a bad sign. She didn't want a relationship. I didn't really want a relationship, but still my eyes would flick round a darkened common room, searching out her wild hair.

Celia kept leaving messages for me. I hadn't arranged to see her again. I was going to, when I got round to it. It was just that I was busy and I didn't think she'd like the places I went that much. I mean she liked bands, but maybe not these bands. And she'd never been much of a party girl. I knew she'd have been home to the village by now and I didn't want to hear about it. She needed to get over it, leave Ash behind. It wasn't normal, all this obsessing. But I'd give her a ring soon. Or maybe I'd go round. That'd be even better. As soon as I had time I'd go round.

One night I was invited to a party in Lorna's block. She met me at the door with a kiss and that was the last I saw of her until about midnight when I found her kissing a bloke called James, who played bass in a band.

'What the fuck.' I couldn't do anything. It wasn't like we were a couple. If I said anything I'd blown it for good. But I'd been counting on staying the night.

I saw Lorna's friend Jenny, leaning against a wall on her own so I went over. She reminded me a bit of Celia, tall, with long hair and a sweet smile. She wasn't that like Celia though. After we'd kissed for a bit she took me back to her room, so I didn't have to walk home alone in the early hours.

Next morning I met Lorna in the shared kitchen. I was drinking milk from the carton, which always helped with hangovers. She was wearing her black silk kimono and in bare feet was tinier than ever.

She raised her eyebrows when she saw me, 'Who did you stay with last night then?'

'Jenny. You were with James I guess?'

'Yeah.' She looked at me with narrowed eyes, then came over and stood on tiptoes in front of me, holding onto my T-shirt to balance. 'I like you David Wilson. Come over tonight, 'bout eight and I'll get some wine.'

'Yeah, ok. If I'm not doing anything else.' I put the milk down and went back along the corridor to bed.

Chapter Thirty-two

One Tuesday evening I'd asked Chi to come round and fill me in on what I'd missed in Macro Economics that morning and we were sprawled on the bed with a textbook between us, when there was a sharp knock at the door.

'Come in,' I yelled. It'd only be Craig asking if I was going down to the bar later.

Celia walked in and I shot upright.

'Celia! I wasn't expecting you.'

'No, I bet you weren't.' She looked pointedly at Chi

Chi smiled back, 'Hi, I'm Chi. Shall we finish this later David?' She started piling her books back in her bag.

'Yeah, ok. I've told you about Celia haven't I? We went to school together.' I turned to Celia, 'And this is Chi. We're both doing Economics.'

They nodded at each other, then Chi slipped out of the room, giving me a wink as she went.

'If this is a bad time I can always come back.' Celia sat down on the foot of the bed.

'It's not a bad time. I just wasn't expecting you.' I got up and put the kettle on.

'Well, your phone's obviously not working so I thought I'd come in person. That wasn't Lorna then?'

'God, no.' I ignored Celia's glare. I'd given up being careful with my language. 'Chi's just a friend. She goes to all the lectures, so I borrow her notes.'

'Never occurred to you to go to the lectures yourself then?'

'Whatever. Did you want something?'

She was straight on her feet, 'Well, I thought you might be pleased to see me. But if I'm interrupting your love life..'

'Chi's a friend, I told you.' No need to tell Celia that Chi had made it quite clear that was all she'd ever be. 'I'm sorry I snapped. Sit down and stay. Or we could go for a walk.'

We went for a walk. It was my favourite kind of autumn day, with a cold blue sky and uncompromising sunlight. We left the student quarter behind and the houses grew bigger and the walls round them taller as we walked. Celia had her hands deep in the pockets of her long black coat or I would have held her hand. I felt suddenly expansive and energised.

'I guess you've been back home then.' I begun. If she wanted to talk, I had time to listen.

'Yeah. I saw Caro. She came round for tea. She said the police have been up at the Hall again. They reckon the Hedley's are running a drugs ring there or something. Apparently there was a big drugs bust in Wales, right around when the Hedley's cleared out.'

'Yeah?' I wasn't in the least surprised. 'Caro tell you about the rows between Ash and his dad as well?' I asked.

Celia stopped and swung to face me, so I nearly ran into her, 'How do you know about that?'

'Dad told me, when I rang home. Said Ash and his dad were yelling at each other for ages, Ash started swearing, then he stormed out.' I looked sideways at Celia, her eyebrows were drawn in a tight black line. 'I was going to tell you. Well, I am telling you.'

She chose to let it go and started walking again. 'Caro mentioned it, yeah. Did your dad say what they were rowing about?'

'No, but let me guess. Ash is out all the time. Ash is drinking too much. He's not turning up to work and when he does he's hung over. Am I close?'

'Pretty much.'

'Just Ash being Ash, without you to keep him in line then.'

'Much worse than that.' She stopped again. 'Ash with Angel to keep him out of line.'

I shrugged and set off again. I liked this bit of the city, where the accountants and barristers lived. I liked to peer through the gates at the houses sprawling across their vast gardens and choose which one I'd have when I'd really made it. Probably the three storey Georgian one with the summerhouse and fishponds. Or maybe the 1920s one with the fancy porch. Celia wouldn't play the game. She'd never choose to live in the city at all. She wanted a house in the country, with an art studio and fields all round. Ash would be there too, a sober, focused Ash. We all need our daydreams.

'Will you go and talk to him then?'

Celia's question startled me out of my reverie.

'Me? Go and talk to Ash? No.'

'Why not?'

'Why not? Oh I don't know. One, I hate his guts. Two, he wouldn't listen anyway. Three, I hate his guts. And four, oh I pretty much hate his guts.'

'Talk to him for me then.' She took hold of my hand and tried to pull me round to face her. I kept walking, let her hand slip out of mine. The days of Celia winning me round were gone.

'Not even for you.' I speeded up a bit and she lengthened her stride to keep pace.

'You don't really hate him do you? You love him, like I do. So do it for him?' She stopped and I kept on walking, quickly, away from her.

Not even for him. Not this time.

Chapter Thirty-three

I hadn't planned on going home at all until Christmas. I wasn't keen on going back then really and toyed with the idea of asking Mum and Dad to come and spend Christmas in the city. We could stay in a hotel and have a posh Christmas dinner and go to loads of shows and pantomimes and things. The only problem was that Mum wouldn't eat a Christmas dinner she hadn't cooked herself. And they couldn't afford the hotel or the shows. And I hated pantomimes. Otherwise it was a good idea.

But then at the end of October, Dad went and broke his ankle. I hoped phoning him would be enough but he sounded really fed up and I started feeling guilty. So I booked a ticket and caught the train home for the weekend.

Mum picked me up from the station and drove me home with a steady commentary on how miserable Dad was and how she hoped I'd be able to cheer him up, how I really should come home more often. I nodded and 'ummd' in the right places and watched the familiar fields unrolling alongside the car. When we got home I glanced casually over at the Old Vicarage but there was no one about and all the cars were gone from the drive.

I'd imagined that Dad would be propped up in a chair, covered with a stripy rug, his leg settled in a nest of blankets whilst he sipped a cup of Horlicks. I'd thought I could sit with him and read stuff out of the newspaper and let him tell me stories from his childhood. I was therefore quite surprised to find that he hadn't aged thirty years overnight and was hobbling crossly round the kitchen with a crutch under one arm and an unopened jar of coffee under the other.

'Hi Dad. How's the ankle?'

'Broken. I hope you've not come home because you're feeling sorry for me. While you are here you can open this jar of coffee.' He thrust the jar at me and hopped over to the kettle.

I offered to make drinks but he waved me away, 'I'm not a cripple. Good job really, left here all day on my own. Not that I'm complaining. I don't want you coming here just to keep me company.'

'Of course he does. We both do,' Mum said. 'He only broke his ankle so you'd visit.' That made Dad grin a bit and we sat round the table with our mugs, while I gave them the edited highlights of the term so far.

After dinner Mum drove Dad down to The Plough for a drink. They wanted me to go with them and I said I might walk down later but I didn't mean it. I wasn't going anywhere Ash might be and anyway I fancied having the house to myself. As soon as they'd gone I stuck the stereo on and crashed on the sofa with a couple of cans and a big bar of chocolate Mum had got in for me. Coming home wasn't so bad, comfy sofa, beer and chocolate, no Mum and Dad.

I ignored the knocking at first. Mum and Dad had a key and I wasn't letting anyone else in. Whoever it was gave up for a bit then started on the window, right behind my head and I nearly jumped off the sofa. Who the hell...?

'Dave! I know you're in there. Open the fucking door, I'm freezing.'

I turned the music up.

'Dave. If you don't let me in I'll break the window.'

I threw the remote down and dragged back the curtains.

'Ash. Piss off.' I went to shut them again.

'Please, let me in, just for a minute. I want to talk.' He had his face right up to the glass. 'Come on, let me in.'

And, fool that I was, I did.

I wouldn't let him in the sitting room, so he sat at the kitchen table, like he used to. He wasn't looking his best. He hadn't shaved in days and his eyes looked out from the dark shadows he always got when he was drinking. There was something else as well, a kind of vagueness in his gaze, a slackness round the jaw. His treasured black leather jacket was dusty and there was a tear in one arm.

He was his usual cocky self though, 'Going to make me a brew then? Or has your dad got some whisky in?'

'You won't be staying long enough for a drink,' I said, 'Did you want to hit me again or was there something else.'

'I told you I was sorry about that. I didn't mean it.'

'It felt like you meant it.'

'Maybe I did, at the time. But I am sorry. Shake on it?' He

held out his hand, slim and tanned and looked at me, his eyes wide with sincerity. I tried to stop something sliding away inside.

I ignored his hand and he shook his head, 'We've been mates too long Dave. Now, get me that drink?'

I met his eyes. 'Ok. But you're not having Dad's whisky.' I passed him the last can out of the fridge.

I shouldn't have let him stay. But it felt like I'd got Ash back and for a while I could forget the other stuff. Even Angel seemed less important. Until he started to talk about her.

She was all he wanted to talk about. I sat there, in my kitchen and listened to my best mate telling me about his life with my girlfriend. I couldn't tell him to stop. Part of me wanted to know, what he'd been doing, where he'd been, who he'd seen, even if it all came back to Angel. He was obsessed. Surely I'd never been that bad. If Angel had fucked me up she was doing an even better job on Ash.

'I don't get her Dave. She's just not like other girls. She just doesn't care about anything. It's great 'cos she doesn't want all the I love you crap but it's hell 'cos she really doesn't care. I could disappear tomorrow and if she noticed she'd be over it by lunchtime.' He stared at his can and I went to get the whisky because I couldn't stand him going on like this. He never talked like this.

'She reckons she's going away and I told her if she does I want to go with her. She laughed at me but I meant it. I'd go tomorrow if she wanted. There's nothing here for me any more.'

'And whose fault is that?' I couldn't resist it.

'I know. But she's like a drug, makes it seem like there's a reason, when there probably isn't.' He shook his head in wonder.

I crumpled my can in my fist, I'd had enough. 'Look, I'm meant to be meeting Mum and Dad at The Plough. Why don't you get back to Angel.' I was unbearably tired. I wanted him to stay.

'Yeah, got to be going,' he said, 'She's got this Halloween thing set up. Apparently it's the Pagan New Year. There's a few of us going to the beach and I reckon it'll be sex and drugs in the sand dunes.' He laughed, all excited now and I thought he was going to invite me along.

'It's been good talking to you Dave. I've missed you.' He got up, hooking his jacket off the back of his chair. I'd missed him.

'Don't come back Ash.'

He flinched as though I'd hit him and a vulnerable look crept into his eyes.

'I mean it. Don't come back here again. For anything. I don't want to know you any more.'

He left without another word and when he'd gone I sat on the kitchen floor and cried.

Chapter Thirty-four

All I wanted was to be left alone to enjoy my new life but the more I tried to put the village behind me the heavier its drag on me became. I told Celia about the scene with Ash and for once she got the message and stopped banging on about him all the time. We met up every week or so for a drink and a couple of times we got student tickets for the theatre. We saw The Crucible and an inexplicable modern play where a huge revolving curtain played a major role. It was nice, spending time with Celia but all the time we weren't talking about Ash, I sensed him in the spaces between us.

The rest of the time I tried to fill my head with sensation so there wasn't room for anything else. I drank too much; I had sex without it meaning very much and as long as I kept it going it was a good place to be.

Dad was still laid up with his ankle, so I had to ring home at least once a week, to see how he was. Grumpy usually. I tried to keep the conversation light but then he told me that Ash had moved out.

'Out where?' Ash had nowhere to go. He'd never go back to his mum or to his grandfather.

'I don't know,' Dad told me. 'There was another blazing row on Sunday night. I tried to turn the tv up so we couldn't hear but your mother said it might be important to listen, in case there was any violence and we had to be witnesses.' I pictured them wrestling over the remote control.

So?'

'So, after about half an hour of Ash and his dad yelling at each other the front door opened and out came John Fitzpatrick with a couple of holdalls. He dumped them on the porch. Minute later Ash came out with Caroline and Kate hanging onto him. He picked up the bags, said something to his dad, who just went inside and then Ash marched off, with Caroline and Kate left crying on the porch. It was horrible.'

'And where is he now?'

'I don't like to ask. I wouldn't like it to look like I was interfering.'

I hated it. The fact that I couldn't let go. However much I tried to shut him out, Ash kept forcing his way back into my thoughts. When Celia found out he'd left home she was distraught. I tried telling her he was an adult, could do what he wanted, that we had both left home but I knew it was different. I thought about going to find him, talk him into going back home but then I remembered what he'd done. He had Angel to look after him now.

When I picked up my post from the pigeonholes and recognised Ash's scrawl across an envelope, I almost ripped it up. But I was too curious, so I took it back to my room to read. To my knowledge Ash had never written a letter before.

Hi Dave,

If you've got this far without ripping it up I'm doing well. I hate writing, you know that, but I've nothing much else to do and I know you wouldn't talk to me. A letter's different isn't it? I'm pretty sure you won't be able to resist reading a letter.

Despite myself, I smiled.

Things got fucked up this summer didn't they? It should have been so good, last summer before freedom. You, me and Celia. You should never have dragged Angel along.

My fingers tightened on the paper, stretching it taut.

She messed you up didn't she? I can see why. She's crazy and not always in a good way. But at least she's around while you and Celia have buggered off into your futures.

I crumpled the sheet between my fingers, then smoothed it out again.

At least you and Celia have futures. You're both the same – you plan, you work hard, you think everything will turn out fine. I hope it does. I'm not like that. It's like Angel says, there's no use making plans, you might be dead tomorrow, just live for now and fuck everyone else. I wish I was like Angel – she squeezes the last bit out of every experience and then she moves on. Nothing matters so why worry? I used to think Celia had it right – she was so calm and so good and she made me feel like I could be those things too. But I can't. There's always part of me wants to break things. Even when I loved her most, I wanted to hurt Celia, just to see what it felt like. Angel understands that. She hurt you enough didn't she?

I wish I was like Angel but I'm not and I've fucked up. Dad kicked me out so I'm staying in the workshops, for now. I don't think further than now. Angel says she's going away and I'd like to go with her. Go away anyway, start again. It feels like things are ending Dave, nothing's that clear any more. I'd like to see you again, just talk, you know, like we used to, good mates.

I'm going to come up to town on Friday. I'll be on the 11.40am train. Lost the Landrover when Dad kicked me out. Meet me at the station Dave and we'll sort things out. Maybe you can get me into Uni with you after all? That'd be great wouldn't it?

So I'll see you about 12.30 on Friday.

Cheers.

Ash.

I folded the letter, smoothed the creases carefully and slipped it back into the envelope. Then I put it inside a book on my shelf and went out.

I never intended to go. I was going to tell Celia, so maybe she could go and meet him, but somehow I didn't. If he'd wanted to see Celia he'd have written to her wouldn't he. Friday I went into lectures with Craig and Chi. We caught the bus and talked about Christmas parties. The holidays started the second week in December and we wanted to pack in as many festivities as we could. I wanted to block out the thought of spending three weeks at home.

We got off the bus at the stop on the edge of campus and Craig headed off towards the engineering block. Chi hitched her rucksack onto her shoulder, 'You coming?'

'Yeah. In a minute. Actually no.' I saw another bus pulling up behind us, with City Centre on its display. 'There's somewhere I've got to be. Take notes will you. I'll catch you later.' I sprinted across the road and swung on board, thrusting my student pass at the driver and waving at Chi, who shook her head and trudged off in the direction of the lecture hall.

I sank onto a seat at the front of the bus and took Ash's letter out of my pocket. He'd be at the station about 12.30. I'd have nearly an hour to wait. I stayed on the bus past the station stop and right into town. It was a circular route and I stayed on through the terminus, as it started the reverse loop. I leaned my head against the window and watched the Friday shoppers moving as one towards the shopping centre, saw the alcoholics and the pigeons in the 1970s precinct; the smart suited lawyers talking fast outside the law courts. All the time I thought about Ash.

There weren't many days went by when I didn't think about Ash. Funny how I had got over my crush on Celia and all I felt for her now was a warm, brotherly affection. I'd even got over Angel, more or less. Lorna proved that. But Ash still had a hold on me. 'You love him don't you?' Celia had said and I'd rushed away because she was stupid and wrong. I didn't love Ash, I hated him. I'd loved Angel, not Ash. How could I love Ash? The bus circled in front of the station and I got up and tinged the bell. The bus staggered to a halt and I jumped off. It was just after twelve. Ash would be here in less than thirty minutes. I must have been hungry because my stomach was turning somersaults.

I bought coffee at a kiosk on the platform and sat on a hard bench. I thought I looked a bit too keen. Like I couldn't wait for him to get there. So I took my coffee up onto the bridge over the tracks. From up there I could see the platform where Ash's train would come in. At twenty five past twelve I had to go to the toilet and as I walked back across the bridge, I saw the train drawing into the station and all the people waiting to catch it rushing alongside as though they could slow it down. I should go down now. He'd be getting off any minute. I put my cup down on one of the joists and leaned out, looking down at the platform. People were getting off, pushing through those trying to get on. I caught a glimpse of a dark head and then he was standing on the platform, stretching his arms over his head and looking round expectantly. The platform cleared and after a few minutes the guard blew his whistle and the train moved heavily away. Ash was still standing in the middle of the platform, looking up and down. After a bit he went and leaned against the wall and lit a cigarette. I drained my coffee and put the cup carefully back on the joist, pushing it into a tight corner so it wedged neatly. Below, Ash must have got bored because he wandered off towards another platform. I hurried back into the gents. I sat down in a cubicle and locked the door. The next train back was in half an hour, another one an hour later. I didn't think he'd wait that long.

When I figured the train was due I let myself out of the gents and went back to my vantage point. I felt light headed, as though I wasn't quite in control. At first I couldn't see him but then, as the train pulled into the platform, he unfolded from behind a pillar. He had a newspaper in his hand and he was still looking round. I wanted to call out, to go down and say 'Ash it's me, I'm here' but I couldn't move. My legs were like glue, holding me in place. He was the last person to get on the train and all the time he was looking, as if I might appear at the last minute. It was only when the doors slid shut behind him and the guard put his whistle to his lips, that my legs unstuck. I pushed away from the wall and pounded across the bridge, down the double flight of stairs onto the platform. The train was moving, sliding away from me and with it Ash. I saw him, sitting slumped against the window.

'Ash,' I yelled and waved wildly. He looked up and he saw me, his eyes widening in recognition. The train was gathering speed.

'Ash,' I yelled again and he raised his hand in a blurred salute as the train carried him back to the village.

'Ash,' I said as my hands fell to my side and the train tail lights winked before they vanished round a corner.

Chapter Thirty-five

I hurled myself into the Christmas season in search of amnesia. I drank until Ash would have been proud of me and smoked marijuana until Chi told me my room was making her high. All I saw when I was on my own or when my eyelids closed, was Ash, climbing onto that train, alone, while I watched from above.

At the Freeman's party I got blasted and crashed in a corner with Lorna and Jenny. James was nowhere around and I wondered which of them I might go home with. Maybe I could go home with both of them. That was something Ash hadn't done. Probably.

'David?' Lorna leaned over and breathed Southern Comfort fumes in my face.

'Uh huh. If you want another drink you'll have to get it. My legs are paralysed.'

'That's 'cos I'm lying on them. Sorry.' Jenny wriggled sideways and the blood flowed back into my legs.

'I don't want a drink,' Lorna went on, ' I only wanted to ask if you were interested in Gavin?'

'Eh? Gavin from Block 9 Gavin?'

'Yeah. Are you interested in him? 'Cos he told me he likes you.'

I was more drunk than I thought. 'Correct me if I'm totally wrong here, but isn't Gavin like, a bloke?'

'Of course he's a bloke.'

'That's what I thought.'

'So, are you interested?' Jenny put in from my left.

'What the fuck!' I turned to look at her. 'Of course I'm not interested. He's a bloke. I'll get you a drink if you want.' I started to get up but Lorna caught hold of my arm and pulled me back down.

'You don't have to be embarrassed. Gavin does like you and I thought it was worth asking. But it's OK if he's not your type.'

'Lorna. What's going on here? Is this some kind of wind up? Gavin seems a nice bloke. But that's just it. He's a bloke. In case you hadn't noticed, I like girls. A lot.'

'I know. But I thought you kind of liked boys as well. I thought …. you know.'

'No, I don't fucking know.' I got up quickly and went back to my room to sleep, alone.

The next day I'd been invited to Celia's Christmas meal. It was a formal affair in Eastlands. A long dining table had been set up in the centre of the huge entrance hall, probably pretty makeshift underneath, but looking the business under a heavy cream tablecloth with proper place settings. The only light was from the candles dripping wax in antique style candelabras. Celia whispered that they'd bought them from the Age Concern shop the previous day but that didn't detract from the air of genteel elegance. It was so completely unlike the Freeman's party I could have been at a different university.

The twelve occupants of the house had each brought a guest and twenty four of us only just fitted around the table. There was a lot of jogging of elbows and muttered apologies as the first course was served. The girls had hired someone's sister and her friends to be waitresses for the night and the sixteen year olds were clearly torn between taking their roles terribly seriously and breaking into giggles. I was as nervous as them, in a hired dinner jacket from Greenwoods. I'd pleaded against wearing one but fortunately Celia had insisted. All the other blokes had DJs. Half of them looked as though they wore them every day and the others were like me, running a finger round the inside of the collar and adjusting their bow ties every five minutes. Celia looked happier than I'd seen her in ages. She was on friendly terms with the other girls from the house now but there was no-one she appeared particularly close to, no-one she turned to or giggled with. Except me. She looked lovely in a black evening dress, long and sweeping with a big slit up the side. Her hair was loose and brushed over to one side.

'Very vampish,' I'd told her when she met me at the door.

She rolled her eyes and said, 'You wish.' But I didn't. Not any more.

The food was OK for a student dinner. The girls had prepared it themselves in the afternoon. Celia told me she was responsible for the carrots and the chocolate sauce. I told her it was an unusual combination but I'd give it a go.

After dinner two of the girls played their cellos and we sat round on chairs and on the stairs, drinking wine. I'd forgotten this was a house of musicians and artists.

'Are you going to show some of your paintings round later?' I asked Celia. We were squashed together on a step, her hair flowing over my shoulder. I played with the glossy strands as the music danced in the spaces around us.

'I'm not putting on a public display tonight,' she laughed. 'I'm exhibiting at the Civic Hall next semester. But I'll show you some stuff I've been doing just for myself if you want to see.'

'Now? Here?' Celia rarely offered to show her artwork.

'Yes. I've been working on these in my room. They're not really part of my college work.'

The piece of music ended and during the ripple of applause we slipped upstairs to Celia's room. She put on the desk light and I sat on the windowsill while she spread half a dozen drawings on the bed. When she was happy with the order she beckoned me over.

They were good, very, very good. I'd only seen a few of Celia's drawings before and these were so much better; the lines stronger, more confident, the use of colour bold and unapologetic. What stopped my breath though was the image of Ash, captured in every drawing. A very beautiful Ash; Ash as he imagined himself, with finely chiselled features, strong cheekbones, eyes you could drown in. But dead. In every single picture Celia had drawn Ash in a pose of death. In one he lay across a bed, reminiscent of Chatterton, outflung hand still gripping the bottle of absinthe. In another he had been stabbed and fell away from the artist with blood staining his perfect skin. In yet another he was untouched but nonetheless dead, cold, perfection in death. I let my eyes roam over the sketches, trying to reconcile the violence and the beauty.

'Well?' Celia was almost nervous, the artist seeking approval.

'You can certainly draw.'

'You don't like them do you?' She pushed me aside and gathered the drawings together, holding them to her chest, like a child.

'I think they're ...'

'Disturbing?'

'Well they are. I mean Ash. Dead.'

'That's what you wanted isn't it. For him to be dead to me. For me to move on. It's figurative, that's all. I'm not going to kill him.'

'I didn't think you were.' I laughed, a little too loudly.

'I shouldn't have shown you.'

'I'm glad you did. They're very beautiful. If only he wasn't so, dead.'

'It didn't work anyway,' she said conversationally. 'I still love him. In fact the more often I killed him on the page, the more I loved him.'

'Oh.' We sat in silence for a while. Then I told her about the letter he sent me; about going to the station but not going to him. That he didn't see me until it was too late.

'So you do love him.' Celia said.

Part Five

Yule

Chapter Thirty-six

I arrived home and walked into Santa's grotto. It was nearly three weeks to Christmas Day but Mum and Dad had overindulged on the decorations. There were streamers I'd never seen before, hanging in the hallway, a real tree in the sitting room and our old artificial one in the kitchen. Tinsel was looped round every picture in the house, including the ones in the bathroom and Christmas carols warbled towards me as I came through the door.

'When did we become headquarters for Christmas?' I asked, dumping my rucksack full of dirty clothes on the kitchen floor.

'We may have overdone it a bit.' Dad followed me in with my other bag.

'We haven't overdone it at all,' Mum said, 'We just wanted to welcome you home for Christmas. Do you want a mincepie?'

'Won't we be Christmassed out by the time it gets here?' I sat down and took three mince pies from the plate.

'Of course we won't. It's just nice to have you home and we want you to enjoy Christmas and not worry about all those other horrid things.'

It would take more than a mince pie and a bit of tinsel to make me forget, but it was a very good mince pie. And it would be nice to have a drawer full of clean clothes for a change.

Celia and I had made a pact. Over the holidays we were going to do our best to rescue Ash from Angel. Put like that, it sounded rather military but it was clear to me now that he needed rescuing. He'd come to me for help and I hadn't given it. It wasn't like I could pretend that I hated him any more. He obviously wanted to break free of Angel and he'd never do it on his own. I didn't think too much about what would happen once we got him away. Celia thought he'd go home and after a bit of adjustment they'd get back together. Maybe they would. Maybe I'd be happy for them.

We certainly planned our campaign like generals. We agreed the first thing was to talk to Ash, let him know we were there. If he was still living in the workshops it was going to be tricky. Angel wouldn't let us just waltz in there and she'd match us move for move. Unfortunately, Ash had always been the chess player.

The campaign received some validation when Mr Fitzpatrick collared me one afternoon. I was on my way to meet Celia and I'd paused to have a good look at the high wall round the Hall. I was considering whether I could climb it. Even if I did there was the risk of the guard dogs or, possibly worse, of running into Angel.

'David. Have you got a minute? David, over here.' A voice called me out of my reverie and I looked round vaguely, finally spotting Mr Fitzpatrick waving from his orchard across the way.

'Hi.' I waved back.

'You got a minute?' he said again and I went over. He was doing something with an outboard engine in the long grass by a pear tree. I leaned against the mossy trunk and watched him. He had long, elegant fingers, like Ash, and the same way with machines.

He unscrewed a part from the engine and handed it to me, 'Hang onto that for me. It's going back in a minute and I don't want to lose it in the grass.'

He normally kept the orchard grass well mown. I held onto the oily part and was pleased I had my old jeans on. He kept fiddling around with the engine and after a bit I asked him if he'd seen much of Ash. He ignored me and gave the engine a firm tap, before straightening up and wiping his hands on a rag. He reached out for the part I was holding and, when I passed it over, he held it in front of him, as if weighing its potential.

'You know he doesn't live here any more?' he said at last and I nodded.

'I won't tolerate drugs in my house, David.' He fixed me with a stern look, 'I've put up with his drinking, with him playing around, but I won't have drugs.'

'Playing around?' The question came out without me meaning to ask it.

'With girls at the boat shows, on the seal trips. You know. I always thought it was a bit rough on Celia but he's too young to get tied to one girl.'

I felt like I'd swallowed bile. Angel was right again.

He'd not been faithful to Celia and I'd never known. My hands clenched into bitter fists by my sides. I hated that Angel was right; hated that he'd cheated on Celia; hated that he couldn't tell me. His dad was oblivious.

'I wish he'd never taken up with that Hedley girl though. You were seeing her for a bit weren't you?'

'Mm.'

'You did well to get rid of her. The wrong sort altogether.' He picked up a wrench and I assumed we were finished. As I started to move away though, he stopped me.

'Hang on a minute. I didn't get you over to talk about the Hedleys. Not directly. When I found out Ashley was messing with drugs I told him to get out. But I thought he'd be back by now, tail between his legs. But instead he's holed up over there.' He gestured towards the wall I'd been planning to scale. 'I'm not demeaning myself going round asking Hedley if I can talk to my own son. But it's different for you. You could go round, ask to see him. He is your best friend.'

'Was.'

'Was. Is. Don't let a little thing like a girl come between you. Go and see him and then come and tell me what he's up to. And make sure he knows I'm here when he's ready to apologise.' And the interview was over. He started banging at the engine with his wrench and I was clearly dismissed.

I walked away, shaking my head. Why did parents, even other people's parents, just assume you would do whatever they told you? And what about Celia? I ought to tell her about those other girls, but then where would the rescue mission be? Maybe I wouldn't tell her. It might not be true. It probably wasn't true. I could tell her when it was all over and we had Ash back. At least now I had a reason to go to the Hall. I was an official delegation from the Fitzpatricks. I had a right to see Ash.

I had no need to assert my rights. The next day, I walked into the village to buy some milk and escape Mum's excessive Christmas spirit. When I came out of the shop I hesitated. There was time for a quick pint before I was expected back for lunch. But we had beer in the fridge. Was it worth the five minute walk round the corner to get handpulled?

As I pondered, a battered blue Volvo pulled up and a head with long, straggly grey hair popped out and addressed me, 'David isn't it?'

'Hm?' It was Philip Hedley. I went up to the car and peered in. He had bare feet, despite the season.

'What are you staring at? It is David. Friend of that idiot I've got in my workshops?'

'If you mean Ash, yeah, I am. Why?'

'Well, I want him out of there. Bloody stepdaughter invited him in. Never asked me. Or her mother. And now I want him out. He's in the way. And he's taking drugs.'

I raised my eyebrows.

'Yeah, well some of us know when to stop. He's not one of them. So can you get him out or am I going to have to get tough?'

Philip was a stringy sort of bloke but he looked strong and there were others. Big Ron was probably still on bail.

I pictured Ash being carried bodily out of the workshops and tipped over the wall outside the Old Vicarage.

'Okay. I can't promise anything but I'll have a word. I'll have to come to the workshops though.'

'Well obviously. Don't disturb the artists.'

And there was me thinking they never did any work.

He gave me a brief nod and chugged away.

Chapter Thirty-seven

The local newspaper came out on a Thursday. The headline the week before Christmas read, 'Two jailed for drugs bust.' Not very poetic but intensely satisfying knowing one of the two was Big Ron. He'd be out in a couple of months but at least he'd miss Christmas. I didn't know the other one named.

The Hall had been searched again. Again the police had found nothing but the villagers reckoned they had the place under surveillance. There were unknown cars parked in the lane at night and casually dressed strangers in The Plough, well outside the tourist season. The Hedleys and the artists appeared to have withdrawn behind the barricades because none of them were ever seen in the village any more. Only the owner of the village shop complained. Occasionally Philip Hedley went forth in the Volvo but otherwise they were lying low. No-one was sure exactly how many of them were living there now.

I thought about Angel. Weeks had passed since I'd seen her. All summer she had been everything and now she was nothing. I felt like I'd had spent a summer steeped in colour and now the winter had bleached it all away, and with it part of who she'd made me. I was afraid to see her again, in case my feelings weren't dead after all. All I wanted was to extricate Ash from her web. To put me and Ash and Celia back the way we had been. Angel could only complicate matters. It was all she'd ever done.

Christmas Day fell on a Saturday. I went to the Hall on the Wednesday before. I didn't tell Celia I was going. I didn't really tell myself. I just got up, downed a black coffee and walked round there without thinking what I was doing. I went straight up the drive, bypassed the house and took the path to the workshops, with my mind completely focussed on seeing Ash. I had no idea what I'd have said if anyone had stopped me.

I found him in one of the unconverted stables. He'd got an old mattress and a sleeping bag and he was out cold. I stood in the doorway and watched him sleep, his arm flung out towards me, his head tilted away. His hair had grown and he was very pale. I went over and knelt by the mattress.

'Ash.' I whispered. Then a bit louder, 'Ash.' He didn't stir. I reached out and moved a strand of hair out of his eyes, letting my fingers trace the contours of his cheek. He murmured and shifted slightly in his sleep. I snatched my hand back. Then I grabbed him by the shoulder and shook him roughly.

'Ash. Wake up you lazy sod. Come on Ash,' I bellowed in his ear and after a moment or two he opened his eyes and groaned.

I looked round the stable. It was bloody cold. A little gas heater in the corner had gone out so I relit it and pulled it nearer.

'How the hell do you live in here?'

He sat up and pushed his hand through his hair, eyes still half closed. He'd slept in his clothes and his black T-shirt was crumpled as he started to button his shirt over it.

'It's not so bad.' He didn't seem surprised to see me. It was like he'd been expecting me. Or maybe he was too stoned for it to register.

'I only sleep here. And eat. Angel brings me food then we go to her room or if Philip's about we go next door.' He nodded towards the other workshops.

'But what do you do all day?' I asked. 'Aren't you bored out of your head.'

'Stoned out of my head you mean.' He laughed, 'No seriously, I just chill out with Angel. And when she's not here I sleep.' Funny, the sound of Angel's name sparked nothing.

'What else is there to do?' He yawned and stretched, arms high above his head. There was a hole in his shirt, right under his arm.

'There's a pan round here somewhere. I'll get some water and make coffee if you like.' He wandered off into the courtyard and I sat on the mattress and waited.

He came back and balanced the pan on the gas cooker. At his direction I spooned instant coffee into a couple of plastic picnic mugs. There was no milk. No sugar. We sat side by side and drank the worst coffee we'd ever had together and it was good.

'What you want then?' he asked. 'My dad send you or were you just nosy?'

'Bit of both I guess. You can't stay in this pigsty forever you know.'

He shrugged. 'I haven't got anywhere else to go.' But there was no conviction in his voice. He knew he could go home.

'I've fucked up Dave.' He'd said the same in his letter. 'Even if I did go home what would I do? I'm not going back to school. I won't work for my family. There's no point in any of it.' He spat the words out like they were poison. 'Seriously Dave what is the point? You're there at Uni, you'll get a degree, a nice safe little job and then what? Get married? Follow Celia round for the rest of your life? Become an alcoholic? Any way, in the end you'll die.'

'Well at least I'm not pissing my life away in a bloody stable and panting after Angel.' I retorted.

'Angel. Now there's someone who gets what life's about.' He smiled and I wanted to punch him really hard.

'Angel's the one who fucked you up mate.'

'I did that myself, a long time ago,' he sounded almost wistful. 'She's the only good thing left. You won't understand but I need her.'

I managed not to say he needed Angel like he needed another drink or another night in that stable. Instead I told him he should talk to his dad. After a bit he said he would, but that he wasn't going home, 'I can't just go back and pretend that everything is clean and pretty and planned. It isn't. It's crap. I've just got to work out how crap. Angel's helping me do that.'

'We could help you. Me and Celia.' In the end I had to force the words out, my throat was so tight with hope.

'Yeah? I saw you on the station.' I met his dark gaze for a long moment. 'Look let me talk to Dad first. See where that takes me.'

I wanted more but he couldn't give it and there wasn't anything else I could say. It didn't feel right, leaving him there. I wanted him to pick up his leather jacket, lying crumpled in a corner, and come with me. I didn't know how to leave. Did he want me to come back? Did I want to come back? And I hadn't told him that Philip wanted him out. I stood up to go and he stood up with me.

'I'm sorry you know. About what's happened. But I can't leave Angel. She knows me, understands I can't live like I used to. It's like all my thoughts are tangled up with hers.'

I knew that feeling.

'I'm glad you came. To the station. And today. I didn't think you would but you came. Despite everything.'

'Yeah.' I looked at him, a long, long look. Then I heard voices out in the courtyard.

'That'll be breakfast,' he said and I turned to go.

'Dave.' His voice half cracked and when I turned back he held his arms out and I went to him and wrapped my arms around him. I pressed my lips into his hair for a brief moment but he pulled away and wouldn't meet my eye.

'I'll catch you mate,' he said and I left hurriedly. I didn't go back down the drive. Instead I found my way through the weeds and brambles to the gate in the wall and pulled myself over with the branch of an ancient apple tree. I sat astride the wall and looked back towards the workshop. I'd seen him, he'd called me mate and he was going to talk to his dad. It was the first step. So why did it feel like it was goodbye?

Chapter Thirty-eight

I had to tell Celia I'd seen Ash. At first she was all wistful and 'I wish I'd seen him.' Then she was full of questions, 'How was he?' 'Did he look ill?' When's he going to see his dad?' 'Did you see Angel?' I told her what I could and let her be all excited and happy. I didn't tell her I thought we were wasting our time. The sight of Ash's prized leather jacket, torn and forgotten in a corner kept coming back to me. And his dad's words, 'I've put up with him playing around' replayed in my head. If we got him back would we know him? Did I even recognise him now? Would Celia?

But for now Celia was happy. And so were Mum and Dad, looking forward to Christmas Day. They wanted us to go to the Christmas Eve carol service together, 'just like we used to.' Possibly, when I was eight and we lived in the city. I didn't ever remember going to the village church at Christmas, but I agreed to go anyway. Celia would be there, we could go for a drink afterwards.

Mr Fitzpatrick was happy too. He waved Dad over Christmas Eve morning, to tell him that Ash had been round. He'd turned up out of the blue while Mr F was at the boatyard and waited with Caro and Kate till he got back. Things had been awkward but not impossible. Ash apologised for bringing drugs into the house. He didn't claim to be clean and his dad didn't ask. Neither of them broached him moving back home but he'd accepted Kate's invitation to go for Christmas lunch. Caro was ecstatic, Kate quietly satisfied and Mr Fitzpatrick was happy. Everybody was happy. I thought I'd better do my best to join in.

Church on Christmas Eve felt right. Obviously it didn't snow but the weather had turned colder and there was frost in the air as we set out, joining a steady stream of villagers down Church Lane. There were a few cars, squeezing past, but most people walked, enjoying the crisp air, the moonlit sky, the sense of expectation. There were lots of little kids, holding parents hands and scuffing shiny shoes in the mud. I hadn't got excited about Christmas for years. Usually I spent Christmas Eve in The Plough with Ash, while we waited for Celia to finish at church then we all caught the bus into Alnwick. We'd get a taxi back in the early hours, usually hammered. Christmas mornings I'd be in a drunken fog, pretending enthusiasm for presents, hoping I could get down enough turkey to keep Mum satisfied. But this year some of my parent's Christmas spirit must have rubbed off on me and I started to feel quite festive.

The ancient building came alive on occasions like this. Dipped in candlelight, with the window recesses and pew ends draped with greenery, the place glowed with a deeper light. I breathed in an atmosphere touched with holiness and I had to blink rapidly. We shuffled into an already overcrowded pew and as I looked round I saw Celia and her Mum, waving from near the front. I waved back and smiled. Then I saw the Fitzpatricks, the three of them and they smiled and waved too and suddenly all the happiness was infectious and I was caught.

The service passed in a nostalgic blend of carols and readings. Children sang Away in a Manger and the vicar talked about charity and welcoming strangers to our door. When it was over I kissed Mum and hugged Dad and said I wouldn't be home late, then I waited in the porch for Celia to emerge from the throng.

She was one of the last to leave. I caught sight of her, deep in conversation with the vicar. She threw back her head and laughed at something he said and her hair rippled darkly in the candlelight. When she came outside her eyes were sparkling and I wanted to hug her and tell her always to look as happy as she did then.

'I've seen Kate and she says she'll ask Ash to call me. You know when he goes round for Christmas dinner? I think he'll listen to Kate don't you?' I nodded. She might be right.

'Come on then.' I tucked her arm through mine. 'Let's go and toast our Christmas.'

The main street was as busy as a summer's day in the holiday season. The local carol singers were out in force, doing last minute business on doorsteps. Families were returning from church or carrying presents round to neighbours. Several people had the purposeful tread which meant they were heading to the pub and we followed them, chattering about our plans for Christmas Day; whether

Ash might join us for New Year. We didn't see the group from the Hall until we almost ran into them.

'Well, David! And Celia. And here was me thinking I wouldn't get the chance to wish you both a Merry Christmas.' It was Angel.

Celia tugged on my arm, trying to walk away but I stopped. I had to. I'd thought I was over it but Angel still had that effect on me. She eyed me with amusement flickering in her eyes. Her hair seemed a little darker, her skin touched with winter pallor but really she was still beautiful. I stood and just looked at her, as if by staring I would be able to work out the source of her power – over me, over Ash – a power that made me want her as much as I hated her.

'Come on.' Celia pulled at my arm again. 'Don't talk to her, she's not worth it.'

'Why so unfriendly Celia?' Angel's voice was mocking. 'I thought you'd be pleased to run into me, so we could swap notes about Ash. Tell me, did he always fall asleep straight after sex? But then, you wouldn't know, would you?' She laughed, turning to her companions, who laughed along. There were three others I recognised from the Hall. The artist Willow, another, younger girl and a man in his twenties, with a ponytail.

'I didn't have to sleep with him to keep his attention, Angel.' Celia's eyes were blazing but her voice was perfectly calm. 'He certainly didn't fall asleep when he was with me. You must be so dull.'

Now I was taking hold of Celia's arm to lead her away. This wasn't getting us anywhere.

'If Ash finds me so dull why can't he keep away from me?' Angel took a step forward, her voice rising dangerously.

'People get addicted to the most poisonous things.' Celia was smiling straight at Angel. 'Luckily, in this case there's an antidote.'

'I suppose that's you is it? Pure, chaste Celia. Balm for Ash's troubled soul.'

'Ash'll be fine when we get him home,' Celia said.

'And that will be when? Last I saw of Ash he was getting ready for the Yule sabbat. We're going to meet him now, go down to the beach, go skyclad and celebrate. Bit more to interest him than your quaint little carol service.'

'You might have Ash tonight but tomorrow he'll be home for Christmas dinner. With his family. Where he should be.' As soon as the words were out I realised I'd made a mistake. Celia's fingers tightened on my arm and a nasty smile crept across Angel's face.

'You reckon Ash is going home for Christmas? I just don't see it happening somehow.' She turned and her cohorts followed her down the street, dipping in and out of the shadows. We stood and watched them go. When they disappeared into the dark, Celia shivered and I put my arm around her.

'Don't let her spoil Christmas,' I said.

Chapter Thirty-nine

Angel didn't spoil Christmas Day. In fact it was one of the best I remembered. I wasn't hung over for opening presents by the tree and, surprisingly, Mum and Dad had bought me what I'd asked for – a new stereo and music. I helped Dad peel potatoes and scrub carrots until Mum chased us both out of the kitchen. We took refuge in the sitting room and sampled the bottle of malt whisky I'd bought him. We played carols during lunch and pulled crackers and wore silly hats. After I'd turned fourteen I found all that stuff a bit lame but now it felt comfortable and traditional, the way Christmas Day ought to be. I washed up with Dad while Mum watched the Queen's speech. We knew she didn't really want to watch it, but she'd never admit it, so we made a play of making sure she was settled in front of the telly in plenty of time.

When Mum started talking about tea, I went up to my room to try out my new stereo. Still stuffed full of turkey and Christmas pudding I winced at the thought of boiled ham, sliced beef, salads, cheeses and four desserts, which would be wheeled out of the kitchen shortly. It was no good protesting it was only three hours since dinner. I lay on my bed admiring the sound quality through my new headphones and wondered whether Ash was getting on OK with his family. I could have gone over, invited him back for a drink but he was probably better at home, putting the pieces back together. Celia and her mum were spending the day, as usual, with her auntie in Dunbar. So I spent a quiet night in, picking at the tea which was left out on the table for hours, 'in case you haven't had enough to eat' and watching mindless, comfortable television. I stayed up after Mum and Dad had gone to bed and finally fell asleep on the sofa, replete with food and drink and Christmas spirit.

Boxing Day my grandparents always came up from Leicester and stayed for a couple of days. I enjoyed seeing them but every year I ended up wishing they wouldn't stay too long. I could only be the perfect grandson for so long before an itch to wear black and spike my hair overcame me.

They were due to arrive after lunch and I was reluctantly helping Dad to bring the camp bed down from the loft, when the doorbell rang. Mum answered and I heard voices outside and then in the hallway.

'The Grand Ps haven't arrived yet have they?' Dad asked, peering out of the window. 'Nope, no car.'

He carried on unrolling the travel mattress, then Mum called up the stairs, 'David. Can you come down a minute please.' I looked at Dad, who shrugged and carried on unrolling.

I went to the top of the stairs and yelled down, 'What is it?' Then I saw Mr Fitzpatrick, standing behind Mum.

Ash hadn't turned up on Christmas Day, hadn't sent a message, nothing. His Dad thought it was another protest,

'Or else he was stoned and didn't dare come near.'

If he'd been out celebrating Yule with Angel that was a real possibility but I didn't think so. Ash had promised to go home for Christmas dinner. He might have wanted to piss his dad off but he wouldn't have done it to Caroline or to Kate. Something wasn't right. I reassured Mr Fitzpatrick that of course I'd let him know if I saw Ash and pass on how disappointed they'd all been, but as soon as he'd gone I dashed upstairs and got my coat. I rang Celia and told her to meet me at the Hall, then I ran, down the lane, through the gates, along the driveway and round to the workshops. I flung open the door to Ash's section. His bedding was in a tangle on the floor, an empty plate and a cup dumped on top. A quick scout round and no sign of his leather jacket. I slammed the stable door behind me and set off running again until I ended up hammering on the ancient door of the Hall itself, yelling for Angel to answer.

Philip Hedley answered the door, took one look at me and disappeared inside again. Before he closed the door on me, I caught sight of boxes and crates. I carried on hammering. I'd knock the bloody door down if I had to. I didn't have to, Angel opened the door a crack and slipped out, pulling the door to behind her. She had on a thin black dress and was shivering. Good.

'What do you think you're doing coming here? You know we don't like visitors.'

'Like I care. Where's Ash?'

'Loverboy's gone missing has he and you want me to help you find him? Can't do that. Sorry.'

'He's not my loverboy.' I was drawn despite myself. She laughed.

'No but you'd like him to be. Wouldn't you?' As she turned to push open the door, I grabbed her arm and yanked her back. Her eyes went dark with shock, then she laughed again.

'Very masterful all of a sudden.'

'Where. The Fuck. Is Ash?' Through gritted teeth. She knew. I knew that she knew.

'I dunno. He might be in the workshops I suppose.'

'He's not. I've looked.'

'Have you been trespassing?'

'What have you done with him Angel? He didn't show up for dinner yesterday.'

'So? Probably didn't fancy playing happy families when he hates the lot of them.'

'He doesn't hate them. He was going to be there. Something's happened.'

She shrugged and wrapped her arms tighter round her body. She was shaking with the cold.

'Last time I saw Ash was down on the beach. He was totally out of it, he doesn't know when to stop.'

'So did he come back with you?'

'No. Look I'm going in now. I hope you find him.'

She put one hand on the door. 'If you try to stop me I'll have Philip set the dogs loose.'

'Set them loose. I'm not going till you tell me what happened to Ash. Where did he go?'

She turned to fix her green eyes on me. For once she looked completely serious and much older than before.

'I don't know where he went. When we'd finished Yule he didn't want to come with us. He was drinking and when we got ready to go he picked up his bottle of whisky and wandered off down the beach. Last I saw he was weaving about towards the sea.' Her voice was flat. I couldn't believe what she was telling me.

'And you left him? You left him on the beach, pissed out of his head, in the dark. God.' I couldn't stop the images, coming faster and faster, piling into my brain.

'Yeah, well, that's what he wanted. Sometimes you've got to let people make their own decisions. Sometimes they actually do know what's best for them. Happy Christmas David.' She went inside and I stood and stared at the door, as if it could somehow tell me what to do. Then I heard the sound of running feet and there was Celia flying up the drive towards me and I was running to meet her and shouting that we had to go, had to get to the beach.

Dad drove us in the end. Celia wanted to get Mr Fitzpatrick but I said no and when I told Dad what had happened he agreed with me.

'Let's just check the beach first. No sense worrying him if we don't have to. Angel's probably made it up to scare you.' But his face was drawn and I knew he was thinking 'What if it was David? What would I do then?' And I wanted to say that Angel doesn't lie. She says horrible things but she doesn't lie.

Dad went one way down the beach and Celia and I went the other. I couldn't think about what we were actually looking for. Celia reached for my hand and I squeezed her mittened fingers. The beach was deserted and we seemed to move across it in slow motion. Above us, clouds drifted silently across the wintry sky. The tide was out and we could see straight away that Ash wasn't there. Still, Dad plodded along the water line and I pulled Celia towards the dunes.

'Let's look up here, they'll have done the ceremony where it's sheltered.'

We found the place almost straight away. Angel had picked the same spot where we'd made love on a summer afternoon, long ago. Did she even remember? They hadn't done a very good job of clearing up.

'I thought they were environmentalists,' said Celia, picking up a beer bottle.

There were lots of bottles, some plastic bags and dog ends of spliffs scattered everywhere. In a hollow between two dunes we found the makeshift altar, a piece of driftwood, with melted candles at each end and a scattering of salt.

'What did Ash want with this crap?' I asked.

'What did you?' Celia replied.

I saw Dad coming towards us across the sand, alone.

'He's not here,' he said. I looked round the dunes one last time and that's when I saw it, pushed behind a gorse bush. Ash's leather jacket, torn, one arm singed. I pulled it from the bush and, wordless, held it out to Celia.

The wheel stopped and with it the seasons. We were frozen forever in winter. There would never be another spring.

They searched the beach for days but they didn't find his body. The police said it must have been carried out to sea on the winter tide.

Mr Fitzpatrick went to the beach every day for a year, searching for his son.

Celia kept the jacket. All through the first days of the search she clung to it like a comfort blanket. I wanted to say, 'who's going to comfort me?'

The Hedley's left the Hall. I don't know exactly when but soon after the lifeboat and the police dogs reached the beach. They must have been packed and waiting inside all the time I was talking to Angel. The police eventually found the cannabis factory, the other drugs paraphernalia but by then it was all far too late.

She must have known she'd killed him, Celia said. From the very beginning she accepted he was dead. Which was better? She knew he was dead and the knowledge cracked her mind open like an egg, while I was still a non-believer, in a world where only faith might have saved me.

Chapter Forty

In the end I went back to University. I had to go somewhere after staying in the village became unbearable. I stayed all the time the real search was on, going down to the beach with Celia, watching the police and the divers, little black figures at the water's edge. We listened to the helicopter blades, whirring out over the sea and all the time I knew that Celia was praying that they'd find him and I was desperate that they did not.

After a week we knew they weren't going to find him and after two they started talking about a memorial service. I wouldn't go. I didn't need to remember him, he was behind my eyelids every time I closed them. I waited outside the church and listened to the hymns and watched the rooks in the empty trees. After the service Celia cracked up. I wasn't surprised, I'd thought she'd been losing her grip for months, ever since Lindisfarne. All those months she'd believed he would come back to her. I couldn't tell her he'd been as lost to her then as he was now. She blamed herself. Because of those stupid, crazy drawings. She'd painted him dead and now he was dead. There was no point arguing with her. One day her mum rang and said that the doctor was admitting her to hospital. She told me the ward number and I knew I wouldn't go. I didn't see myself visiting the psychiatric ward and watching Celia weave baskets and weep for Ash. I sent flowers and my mum. And I went back to University.

I'd missed nearly four weeks of term but it felt like I hadn't missed anything. It was all so perfectly, wonderfully normal. Someone must have explained to my housemates what had happened but they didn't talk about it and neither did I. I ignored the sympathetic sideways glances and soon they stopped. It was much easier for everyone if we pretended that tragedy had never happened. It might be contagious. So keep it locked away in a box. With honesty and guilt and the love that refused to speak its name. Until it was too late.

Chi lent me her notes and I made a pretence at catching up. I guessed the lecturers would go easy on me. I needed careful handling, might require counselling. Lorna avoided me and I avoided Jenny, who might have said all the right things. Instead, a couple of nights after I'd got back, I searched out Gavin.

He was leaning against the bar in the Junior Common room, talking to the student barman. Ash would have volunteered for that job if he'd ever made it here. They both looked up and I ordered a beer.

'Can I get you one, Gav?' I offered. He looked surprised and pleased and when the drinks came I signalled that we should take them over to a table in the far corner, out of sight of the bar. I had no idea what I was doing.

I knew Gavin a bit through Lorna. Which was how I knew he was gay and that he fancied me. What else did I need to know? I guessed he was more experienced than me at these things. I put my glass down, smiled at him and let him take it from there.

After I left his room, sometime around midnight, I went out into the square and sat on a stone bench. I lit a cigarette and looked up at the stars. I didn't feel any different. I didn't know what I'd expected. Some sort of revelation, a blinding light, to say this is the future, this is who you really are. There was none of that, just some soreness and a feeling of detachment. I watched the clouds tangling around the crescent moon. My feelings seemed as distant as the barren planet. I thought about Ash and it didn't hurt. That was the trouble, it ought to hurt. I wanted it to hurt. That was the problem with Gavin. He just wasn't enough like Ash for me to care.

Part Six

Beltane

Chapter Forty-one

Five years later

The encounter with Gavin set the pattern for the next few years. I finished my degree, ending up with a bare pass and only went to graduation to please my parents. They've got the official photo up in the sitting room, the pair of them grinning at either side of me and me looking at the photographer with a challenge in my eyes. I can't remember if he took me up on it.

I got a job through my dad, who rightly decided if he didn't sort something out I'd do nothing for myself. Except see a few more bands, shag a few more men, or women. Dad didn't know about that bit of course. I started as an accounts trainee in a firm of Management Consultants in the city centre. That was my only stipulation, I had to stay in the city. Now I had my anonymity back I wasn't giving it up again for the spotlight of a small community. The idea – Dad's and the company's – was that I'd work hard, pass my exams and become a chartered accountant. But what would have been the point? In five years I've progressed only because everyone senior to me has left. The job numbs my brain but I earn enough to pay for my flat, my gigs, my fags and my drink. If I want any more there's usually someone who can supply it. Why would I want to start studying again? What would it be for?

In five years I've hardly been home. Mum and Dad come to visit me and if I have to go back, like when my gran died, I keep the visits short. I refuse to go The Plough and keep my bedroom curtains shut so I don't have to look across at the Old Vicarage or see the high wall snaking round the Hall. It's deserted now, falling back into disrepair and I'm glad.

That's my life, crap job, crap flat, a lot of meaningless sex and some pretty meaningless bands mixed up with the good ones. It took me a couple of years to realise it was the perfect way to keep up the search. For me Ash was never dead. And Angel still has the answers. So in every face and every body I touch, I am looking for them.

And then I go to that gig. It's one of my favourite bands, one I've seen many times before, in venues all over the north. Their songs of pain and defeat, wrapped up in achingly beautiful melodies touch places I thought were dead. The gig is on a Friday, work behind me for forty eight blessed hours and I give myself up to the pleasure of expectation, waiting for the band and the first unmistakable crash of chords. It is then, as the band finds the first perfect note and the crowd swoons with the hit of the familiar chorus, I see her. I haven't seen her for over five years, didn't know her well even then but there is no mistaking her waist length hair, her stupid mystical expression, the hardness of her eyes. Four maybe five people away from me, half hidden by the crowd, I am looking at Willow. Wind painter, drug taker, Hall dweller, best friend of Angel. And so it all changes. The vague, unspoken mission to find her crystallises and by the time I wake up in Willow's bed I am halfway to having a purpose in my life again.

Willow doesn't want to talk of course. When she realises who I am, in the cold, uncompromising morning light, I see something like fear in her eyes. I guess I've changed more than she has since I saw her last, laughing in the Christmas moonlight, waiting for Angel, so they could take Ash down to the beach and away from me. She sits on the edge of the bed and reaches for a robe to cover her breasts. It's her flat so she can't leave. I don't want to frighten her. Whatever she has done, the only thing I want from her is information.

'Where's Angel?' I keep my voice calm and low.

'I don't know what you mean.' But there's a question in her voice and I stare incredulously, so she quickly shrugs and says instead, 'I don't know where she is. I haven't seen her for years.' Which we both know is a lie.

I settle back onto the bed, hands behind my head and prepare to wait her out. I won't threaten or harangue, just wait until she tells me and then I'll go. I remind her that the police are still keen to close the file on the drugs ring at the Hall, that they would welcome names and addresses, any names and addresses, of those who were there then. I say it looks like she has a nice flat, a nice life and she says she doesn't want to move again, that she's settled here. I tell her fine, all I want is an address. And finally she gives it to me. I look at the scrap of paper and insist on comparing it with the address book she's copied from. I recognise Angel's own slanty scrawl. She's back in Wales, in Anglesey this time. I thank Willow and tell her that's all I want and she looks at me with her head on one side as if trying to weigh me up. Then she offers me a coffee and I say no but we part on good terms and if I go back to her flat it won't be for information.

Before I go to Anglesey there are things I need to do. After all this time suddenly there is no rush at all. I ring Mum and Dad and tell them I am coming home for the weekend. I ask Dad to speak to his estate agent friend, the one who is overseeing the sale of the Hall and I ring Celia, in Harrogate, and ask her to come home.

Chapter Forty-two

Though they try not to show it Mum and Dad are delighted to have me home. Even as Dad shakes my hand and Mum asks casually if I've had a good journey I can feel the fizz of excitement that I'm here. And I feel a little corresponding fizz. I miss them, it's not them who keep me away. Dad comes out to look at my car. Passing my driving test has been one of my few achievements these last few years. A car is useful for travelling to distant gigs and now for tracking down Angel. Then we go and sit with Mum and drink tea and the only sign that I'm not a regular here is the visitors teapot.

When Dad takes my bags up to my room I follow him.

'Are you staying long this time?' As though last time was only the other week.

'Just a couple of nights,' I say.

I have to stay in my old room. There isn't anywhere else. It's always a shock to find it just as though I'd popped downstairs for a drink, or been out to the pub with Ash. My desk is tidy, mum's influence, but my pens are stacked at one side and my pile of notebooks at the other. I could slip into the swivel chair and start my homework. Most of my books are still weighing down the surprisingly robust shelves Dad put up when we moved. I go across to the window and sit on the wide sill, where I can look into the lane. And God it hasn't changed. It hasn't changed at all. The wall still snakes round the boundary of the Hall, the door's still half choked with ivy and across the way the Old Vicarage glowers in the sunlight, just the way it always did. There's even a car pulled up in the drive with a surfboard on the roofrack and a line of washing moving slowly between the apple trees. I've slipped back in time and I have a weight of tears inside that I can't let go. Not yet. Not here. I go downstairs and ask Mum to tell me everything she's been doing since I was home last. Tell her not to leave out a single detail. She beams and the dam inside feels more secure.

Dad hands over the key to the Hall with a warning not to let anyone see me. His friend has done him a favour but they can't let everyone in to have a look. I think he'd like to come with me but knows better than to ask. I thank him for the keys and clasp his shoulder as I go out.

The key for the side gate is missing so I trudge up the driveway, my legs growing more reluctant with every step. There are weeds growing through the gravel drive and when I reach the Hall, the steps are choked with last autumn's leaves. I fight with the ancient lock and push the massive door open. In all those months with Angel she never once invited me inside the Hall.

In many ways it's like my first view of the workshops – disappointing. It is after all just a tired old Hall which may once have been grand but now is verging on dereliction. The £1 million price tag seems forlornly

258

optimistic. The Hedleys were the last family to occupy it but they have left few traces of their stay. The rooms are mostly empty, save for some decaying curtains and a pair of red, high heeled shoes in the middle of one large room. Angel's? I think for a moment before I recognise that she would never, ever have worn red stilettos. No, probably Sylvia's. I could picture Lady Hedley in red high heels.

I take the central staircase to the first floor. The carpet has been rolled up and I see that this is quality workmanship. Solid oak stairs, wide and shallow with an ornately carved balustrade, which coats my fingers with dust as I run them along the grain. Shame they've been so badly used. Scuffs and gouges pockmark the wood all the way to the broad, square landing at the top and there are deep scratch marks as if someone had vented their spleen. Angel? I think again and this time I can picture it.

I find what must have been her bedroom. It's not like it has her name on the door but I can tell just the same. For a start there is still the lingering trace of incense in the air. Say I'm imagining it. That it can't have persisted all these years. But I can smell her incense, know her scent.

I find a crystal by the window. Anyone else might have missed it. But I find it, a slim black stone, obsidian I think, wedged between the sill and the frame. How do I know it's Angel's? Because she was the only one who would carry a black crystal. Cut her and she'd bleed black.

I'm standing by the window, turning the stone over and over, trying to conjure up the girl who left it behind, when I hear the front door slam and the sound of footsteps on the stairs. She's on time. I push the crystal into my pocket and go to meet Celia.

It's not strictly true to say that I haven't seen Celia in five years. We've met. A couple of times when she came out of hospital, once when she came into the city to see me and once at the police station. They called us in when they were winding up the investigation and we had to review our statements and sign something to say we'd pass on any further information we came across. Each time we've met has been more awkward than the last. I don't really understand why. Surely we should have turned to each other when Ash disappeared and then gone on without him. The fact that Celia's convinced that he's dead and I'm still searching doesn't help but it's probably more that without Ash there's nothing to hold us together.

So we greet each other warily. I hold out a hand but that's far too formal so I lean in and kiss her cheek and she doesn't pull away.

'Why here?' she asks, straight away. We're standing in the big entrance hall, which is completely empty and echoes eerily.

'I don't know.' I tell her honestly. 'It felt like the right place. Where the trail went cold.'

'The trail?' and instantly she's wary and I can tell she thinks I'm going to bring up the whole, Ash might still be alive thing.

'Angel's trail. I've found her.'

Silence. Celia turns and starts walking towards the door. Then she stops and turns back to me.

'Where?'

And we go into the old drawing room and sit on the empty window seat and I tell her all about the concert and Willow and I show her the address.

'Can we trust her do you think?' she asks and I tell her yes. Then we leave the house and lock the door behind us. I ask if she wants to go and see the workshops but she shakes her head and we leave together.

Chapter Forty-three

It's a long way to Anglesey so we share the driving. It's surprisingly relaxed in the car. We take it in turns to choose the music and criticise each other's taste. We stop at service stations and eat takeaway food and drink coffee from cardboard cups. We fill the car with sweet wrappers and I start to feel I'm in an American road movie. Anyone seeing the two of us bopping along the motorway would never guess at the real reason for our journey.

We stop overnight in a village outside Chester. I've found an ad in a paper for a pub with rooms but haven't thought to ring through and they're full. The landlord directs us to a B and B, a couple of hundred yards away. We take the vacant room and go to bed in matching pink beds. I don't sleep much and from the sighing and turning from the other side of the room, I guess that Celia isn't faring any better. I think about holding her.

Lying awake in the dark always exaggerates my fears and now the thought of simply driving into Wales and confronting Angel seems ludicrous. What are we going to say? 'By the way, did you actually kill Ash or just stand by and let him drown?' I turn my pillow over for the hundredth time and force my eyes to close in an attempt at sleep.

To while away the miles, we speculate in what sort of place Angel will live. Guesses range from a Romany caravan to a tepee to a high rise flat. We discount the latter as soon as we drive over the old Menai Bridge onto Anglesey. No high rise flats here, only an unfolding of small fields between crumbling stone walls and white croft cottages under a high, pale sky. It is beautiful but alien to me and I can see why Angel brought her paganism to this Celtic landscape.

Neither the landscape nor our many guesses prepare us for the neat white bungalow with a conservatory and manicured lawn in a pretty seaside village.

'You've got the wrong address,' Celia says straight away. 'Angel won't live in a place like this. It's positively middle class.'

I check the bit of paper again - Tralee, Cliff Road, Treadur – then the name on the side of the bungalow.

'This is it. I checked it in Willow's address book. She didn't have time to change it.'

Celia shrugs and we both get out of the car. Now we are here we're both at a loss, unsure how to proceed. I have the crazy thought that we should have brought flowers and a bottle of wine.

'Come on then. As we're here.' Celia leads the way towards the front door. There are herbs growing along the path, lavender and rosemary and as we get closer I see a dreamcatcher, hanging in one of the windows. Maybe it is the right place after all.

Celia knocks on the door, uncharacteristically bold, and then we hold our breath. In the seconds before the door opens the reality that I might be about to see Angel hits me and sets thoughts spinning through my head like the colourful sails on a child's plastic windmill. Angel kissing me in the moonlit workshops; Angel in scarlet at the Lammas sabbat; Angel in the barn, naked and soft beneath my touch; Angel at the party, dancing with me, dancing with Ash, kissing him. And then the door opens and she is here.

'Hello David, I've been expecting you.' And her lips curl in a familiar half smile, 'but Celia as well. Now that's a surprise.'

'You might as well come in. You've driven a long way. And quicker than I expected. I had you down to arrive tomorrow.' Willow, I think, recognising we've lost our one advantage

We follow her into a wide hallway, full of children's toys and on into the conservatory.

'Make yourselves at home. I suppose you'll want drinks.' She doesn't wait for an answer and Celia and I perch on delicate cane furniture and try not to look round too obviously.

'How come she's living here?' Celia hisses across at me.

'Because she was invited to.' Angel comes back in with three bottles of lager on a tray. 'I take it you both still drink.'

We nod and take tentative sips.

'You remember Big Ron?' she asks.

'Yeah.' I reply. How could I forget.

'This is his ex wife's house. She bought it with the divorce settlement.'

'How the hell did Ron get enough money to buy this?' But then I remember. Drugs. And Angel gives me a conspiratorial wink.

I keep glancing at her, trying not to stare. She's not changed, not really. Her eyes are as watchful as ever. Her hair still long, pulled into two braids. She's wearing a long grey dress with purple slashes, and bracelets which chime gently when she moves. But yet she has changed. Her face is older, more set and there's a stillness I don't remember, like she's found her centre. She senses me watching and fixes me with one of her penetrating gazes.

'You've come to ask about Ash. I've been expecting you for five years, I'm only surprised it took you so long. I've moved about a bit but still, an important matter like that.'

Celia is tensing and I try to diffuse them both.

'We just want to know what happened the night he disappeared. I know what you told me at the time but you wouldn't have just left him to drown. Not even you would do that.'

'Not even me?'

'But you did, didn't you Angel?' Celia's voice is very low and too tightly controlled. 'You knew you'd lost him. He was coming home for Christmas and you couldn't bear it. You might not have held him under but you killed him just the same.' She's shaking and whilst I know that all her grief is finally finding a focus, it isn't helping.

'I don't think you did kill him Angel. But I think you know what happened.' I try to put all my aching loss into the look we exchange but she just shakes her head.

'I don't know what happened. I told you all I knew back then. He was drunk, he was stoned, he stayed on the beach. It was his choice, I couldn't force him to go. He probably drowned. In fact I'm sure he did. It was sad but it wasn't my fault and you have to let him go.' She is so calm, so still.

'I can't let him go,' I say softly and when she looks at me there is a warmth in her eyes that I can't fathom.

'You killed him.' Celia is on her feet and bearing down on Angel, who doesn't move to get out of the way. I try to step between them but then there are quick footsteps and a little figure throws itself towards Celia.

'Leave my mama alone. Nasty lady, leave her alone.'

Celia stops dead and her hand creeps slowly to her mouth. I follow her gaze to where Angel is seated, calm as the Madonna with a little boy at her side. He must be about four or five and when he turns his head I see what has made Celia crumple into her chair. From his mother's knee the little boy looks back at me with the clear dark gaze of his father.

Chapter Forty-four

'This is Seb. My son,' Angel says proudly. 'He's the reason I'm living here. It's not too bad, there are plenty of Pagans around. Did you know Anglesey was one of the main seats of Druid power in the Dark Ages?' If I didn't know her better I'd think she was talking to give Celia time to compose herself. Seb watches solemnly as Celia wipes her eyes and tries to steady her breathing.

'He's Ash's isn't he?' Her voice is ragged, ripped raw.

'Can you go and play in your bedroom for a little bit?' Angel says to Seb. 'You can finish that Beltane drawing for Rowena.'

'What about the nasty people?' he asks.

'They'll be going in a little while and they're quite safe, but if I need you I'll shout really loudly. Is that OK?' She takes his hand and leads him out of the conservatory. She still has the capacity to amaze me.

When she comes back she sits on the edge of her chair and addresses herself to Celia.

'I'm sorry you had to find out. You won't believe me but I really am. I don't get off on hurting people so much these days.'

'Did Ash know?' I can't believe how much hurt there is in Celia's voice. She stares as if Seb was still in the room and she was drowning in his eyes.

'No. I didn't know myself till about three months later, when we got back to Wales. And he's my son, no-one else's. Ash being his father is just an accident of paternity.' She looks at me then and I realise that he could have been mine. All those times together, that solemn little boy could have been looking back at me with my eyes. But of course Ash won that one too.

'Do you tell him about Ash?' Celia asks and I'm amazed to see some kind of light waking in her eyes.

'Of course.' Is all Angel says but they exchange a long, long look and I sense messages passing between them that I can't begin to fathom.

'I think it's time to go, David.' Celia starts to get up. 'She can't tell us anything. Ash is dead but at least there's a beautiful little boy who'll grow up knowing what a wonderful man his father was.'

'I don't want you to contact us again,' Angel says.

'I won't,' Celia replies and again that long look. 'I'll wait in the car.'

Left alone with Angel I sense again that she has changed. Something has softened.

'It's better that she accepts he's dead,' she says to me. 'Imagine if he hadn't died and he'd just walked away. From her. From his family. From almost everyone who loved him. Imagine if he let them believe he was dead, and left them to mourn for all that time, never sending a word to say that he was safe. Imagine how betrayed she would feel.'

'Imagine.' I say and never take my eyes from her face.

'He loves his son though', she says. 'He might be a lousy human being but he does keep in touch with his son.' And she is pushing a bit of paper into my hand.

'It wasn't all bad was it?' she says, 'You and me?'

I look at her and half smile. Then I shake my head, 'Goodbye Angel.' And this time it really is.

Chapter Forty-five

I stuff the bit of paper into my pocket without looking at it and join Celia in the car. We sit in silence for a minute then I start the engine. I'm not ready to start the long drive home, so I pull into the car park of a big pub, about ten minutes from Angel's house, overlooking the sea. The place is almost deserted on a Tuesday lunchtime and we sit in a big bay window and look down at the beach. The tide is up and seagulls ride the waves towards the shore. I'm reminded of all the times we ate lunch overlooking the sea in the old days, me and Celia and Ash. We order and wait for the food to arrive. I keep turning over Angel's words and finger the piece of paper in my pocket.

'I wish it had been me.' The small voice breaks into my thoughts and ashamed I turn to Celia. She's looking out to sea, twisting a strand of hair round and round her finger.

'It should have been me. Having his child. I was the one who loved him. Angel never did. And yet she's got his child.' She starts to cry and I put my arm round her shoulders and pull her close. Then the food comes and she pulls away, sniffing and pushing her hair out of her eyes.

We eat in silence but when the meal is over and our plates cleared away she says, 'I don't regret not sleeping with him you know. Even now. I loved him but I loved God. I still love God. And so I know that he's safe, in heaven.' Her eyes are shining but softly, none of the fanatical glow I've seen before.

'It's nice there's another Ash. I mean I'll never see that little boy again and I don't think I'll ever forgive Angel but I can think about Seb growing up and knowing about Ash. It's like he has a second chance at life.'

All the way home, as Celia sleeps, I think about that. Ash having a second chance at life. Celia said Angel didn't love him. But Angel had given him something none of us could have done. Not the child. But his freedom. She'd helped him go away, leave us behind, make a new start. Could I have done that? Let his father go on searching the beach day after day? Seen Caro crying at her window? And said nothing? Could Celia?

I think about seeing him again but I still don't look at the address. I can't bear to see whether he's been living an hour's drive away from me all these years. Or maybe he's in the Scottish isles. He'd always wanted to go to the Hebrides and I picture him now, living in a tiny croft by the sea, with a boat drawn up on the sand outside. I try to picture myself there with him. His face when he sees me and disbelief turns to delight. How much will he have changed? Is he still drinking? Will I feel the same? All the time I'm driving I see his pale skin, his dark eyes, the lock of hair that falls across his face.

I drive all day and it's evening when we reach our turn off the A1. The nights are long now and the sun only just beginning to decline.

Celia wakes up and looks around, 'Are we nearly home?'

'Yeah. Not far. Do you mind if we take a brief detour?'

She shakes her head and I drive past the village turn and on towards the coast. I park at the top of the beach path.

'I won't be long,' I say and get out and walk down through the dunes onto the beach. I pass the place where Angel and Ash celebrated Yule, the night he disappeared and go on, down to the water's edge. Out of the corner of my eye I see that Celia is following me but it doesn't matter. I take the piece of paper Angel gave me out of my pocket. It is folded and deliberately, without unfolding it, I tear the scrap into tiny pieces. Then I scatter them into the wind. Some catch the breeze and swirl out to sea, others fall onto the wet sand and are soon collected by the incoming tide, lapping at my feet.

'Goodbye Ash,' I call to the setting sun and the wind takes my words and carries them to Celia. She walks towards me, beautiful, loyal Celia, who never let me down. Celia, my best friend. She puts her arms around me and rests her cheek against mine. I smell the sweetness of her hair.

'Can you let him go now?' she asks. 'Can you finally accept that he's dead?'

Imagine that he just walked away. From everyone who loved him.

I tighten my arms around her.

'Yes,' I say. 'I can let him go now. For me, Ash is dead.'

In a while we walk back up the beach, hand in hand. The sun is slipping beyond the horizon. It is the start of the summer.

THE END